The Naked Law
Linda Joyce Ott

ISBN 978-0-9865836-7-4 (print edition)

Published by GUNLIN
144 Holton Ave. S., Hamilton Ontario Canada L8M 2L5

For Günter, Carl & Stefan

.

The Naked Law

Naked you came into this world,
naked you must leave it.

Part I

In the Middle of Things

I woke up early this morning, lay in bed staring at the light peeping in through the blinds, and decided that I would start a blog. Just like that - with no business plan, no outline and no strategy. I felt a calling to just do it.

And I knew what I would name my blog. It had to be *In the Middle of Things* - that is as long as no one else had that domain. I toyed with *In Media Res*, the Latin version, but decided that in keeping with *The Naked Law* I would be clear and use plain old English.

Made myself a pot of java and dragged my ass to the chair. It was really simple to sign up for a blog. Free, too. Before I finished my first cuppa, I had secured *In the Middle of Things* as my handle and registered it as a dot-com.

My big rock done for the day. Tick that off.

I could do nothing else today and still feel as if I had accomplished something.

So I prowled about my crib looking out the windows to see what the day was like. As if I could tell anything from way up here. I trolled for a bit. Checked the weather, read the headlines, clicked messages and took a shower. Stretched out for a while.

Another hit of joe and I was back, ready to launch.

What's this?

Insert tagline and description, so that your viewers know what your blog is about.

You & Me & The Final Catastrophe. Life after The Great Resolve. Lives under The Naked Law Revealed. 1,001 Stories of the Unpossessed. The History and Future of Things.

Perhaps though I should pick a design first. Something journalistic and visual. Classy and bold. But not over the top. Minimalist. Just a click and I would have it.

Except it doesn't quite work out that way. Hundreds of graphics. Upgrades galore. Another decision needed.

Hit sleep. Gotta step back before going forward.

Setting Up a Blog for Dummies. OK. A little break and here I am again, AIC.

For as long as I can remember, I've been fascinated with the decadent world before *The Decline*.

All that out-of-control overconsumption and rampant consumerism. And the blatant disregard not only for the environment, but for every living thing in the world. Trees, bees, butterflies, cows, chickens. The soil. The water. The air. You name it. Devastation everywhere.

And it's not like people didn't know. The writing was on the screen. Had been for decades. Shoot. Those people were our parents, our aunts and uncles, our grandparents. But who were they in fact?

I needed to find out what they were thinking back then and how they are feeling now. I wanted to hear stories from folks who lived during *The Decline* and survived *The Final Catastrophe*. How are they coping in our brave new world?

How are they managing their lives under *The Naked Law*? How are they hacking it without their precious things?

I guess my blog could be a clearing house for reports from the frontlines. And maybe, all of that shared knowledge and insight would turn into a grow-op of similars coming together to embrace some ultra-rad notions.

In the Middle of Things would be my online café where anyone could drop by for a chat, rail a bit, learn a few things, pick up some interesting news, and follow some links.

So, as they used to say, without further ado …

Hello and welcome.

My name is Steve Discony. I'm just one more journalist who thinks that he's got a book in him and is setting up a blog to explore some ideas. Join me if you like. I don't know where this adventure will go, but it should be a trip.

A Chorus of Voices
B. K. Reacts to an Email Missive

Hello blogsters. I won't tell you who passed on these intriguing anecdotes, but I'll present them occasionally as I come across them. Here's the first one:

Hey Steve, I'm so glad that your blog lets people share some of the incredibly asinine dictates of our nanny state. Here's an email that I just received from the bureaubats.

"Forfeiture Notice

"Pursuant to the fact that you eat on average ten of your 21 meals a week at registered dining facilities and supplement the remaining meals with take-out food five to seven times a week, the authority is granted to us to demand that you forfeit the following items: one (1) counter-top stove, one (1) oven and one (1) full-sized fridge with freezer component, as well as, but not limited to, any pots, pans and other cooking utensils that you use with the above mentioned items.

"You have thirty (30) days to comply with this order and dispose of the items in a legal way following the rules and regulations of *The Act for the Lawful Disposal of Goods and Property Forfeited* by directive of the Department against Overconsumption.

"If necessary, you may replace the full-sized fridge with freezer component with a bar-sized fridge without freezer component. To do so, apply using the form - Replacing an Item Forfeited by order of the Authority of the Department against Overconsumption.

"On your application form, you must fully complete the details on why you need the replacement item and have it witnessed. Note that relatives sharing your dwelling may not act as witnesses for the purposes of this form. Attach an electronic copy of this email to your application.

"Be advised that we use surveillance and tracking tools judiciously, and only if we suspect that you are not totally upholding one or another of the 1,666 laws that govern the United Entities of the World (UEW).

"If you wish to contest the results of our surveillance and tracking as per *The Bylaw Rescinding Your Rights and Giving Approval for Tracking in the Case of National Security*, you may fill out form CST6848rrz - Contesting Surveillance and Tracking by the Authority."

So Steve, because they tracked my dining habits (which I will admit weren't particularly frugal - loads of restaurant meals and take-out food), they're demanding that I get rid of not only my pots and pans and cooking utensils, but also my stove and oven. And I have to scale back to a bar-sized fridge.

When I called about it, the VRs said that my consumption and purchasing habits showed that those appliances and utensils were surplus to my needs. Therefore, I was misusing my personal dwelling space allotment and the items could be better utilized by others.

Do you believe it?

Now if I wanted to cook, I can't. I'm stuck managing with just the microwave. This is making me physically sick.

How can I eat healthy without a stove, oven and fridge?

I know that I haven't used the oven in years, but I might need to and then what?

Jeez, I hate the way this regime just rides roughshod over everyone. They do not understand that you could change your habits, or that circumstances might force you to do things differently.

OK, OK, I know you don't simply transform your routine but it's the principle that's the issue, isn't it?

Like what if I was laid up and couldn't go out of my apartment, how would I cook healthy then without a stove? Or what if I was snowed in?

Even if I didn't use the freaking stove and oven, it gave me a sense of comfort to have them there, just in case. Same thing with the refrigerator. I can't prepare large quantities of food and freeze them with a crappy mini-fridge.

But obviously, they really don't like you storing anything anyway, do they?

Yeah, I forgot that saving is a sin now. I remember when it was a virtue. Save for a rainy day. A penny saved is a penny earned. Now everything's use it or lose it.

What really irks is that the spies are all over the place monitoring every purchase that you make - watching what you do, where you go, and now even, what you don't do.

So Steve, you can see that, like your blog, I'm caught in the middle of things.

I don't like to tackle with Big Bro, but I want to fight for my rights. And I don't think that this is fair at all, so I'd appreciate any advice you or your followers can give me.

Qs & As from the Clutter-Buster's Blog

Hey bloggos, I've got a treat for you today. Amy Anderson, author of The Clutter-Buster's Manifesto, has given me permission to re-blog Qs & As from her site.

Here's a recent post:

Dear Clutter-Buster:

Recently a couple of friends were at my place for lunch. After a few glasses of wine, one of them began lambasting *The Naked Law* and "all its incredibly stupid rules and regulations prohibiting our most basic human freedoms."

While this angry outburst was bad enough among adults, young children were present. What should I say to my friend and to my daughter and her playmates? Should I maintain this friendship? I am genuinely distressed, but my husband tells me to just ignore it. - *upset in Utopia*

Dear Upset in Utopia:

Why didn't you interrupt this rant while it was going on?

That action alone on your part would have communicated so much to your impressionable child and to her friends. You would have shared with them not only your approval of the law, but also your proficiency in rational discourse.

Stopping the tirade as it occurred would ensure that your protest is what the children would remember most from the awkward incident. It would also have given them a valuable lesson in dealing with obnoxious people.

As well, it would have conveyed to your friend that her criticism of the law was objectionable right at the moment it was happening. Confronting her after the incident is less effective as it leaves open the possibility of her denying what she said and accusing you of over-reacting.

It could also lead to further arguments along the lines of "what I said and what I meant" that probably could not be amicably resolved and that would most likely lead to the end of the friendship.

Sheri Does the Inventory Her Way!

Hi Steve. I just want to rant a bit on your blog about filling out the Essential Goods Inventory form. It's not that I object to *The Naked Law*, it's the limitations of the form itself that disturb me. And I'm not just spouting off. I have my day in court scheduled.

Yep, I get to argue the case against the inventory form. And I will use my line of reasoning and anything that you and your followers might add to try to get the apparatchiks to revise the damn document.

Here's my gripe. The Essential Goods Inventory form, which, as you know, absolutely everyone has to complete or risk hefty fines or imprisonment, doesn't allow you to go into any detail about the items that you own, the things that you cherished and held on to over the years.

It doesn't let you relate how you found the piece in the first place - which is often a great story in itself.

It doesn't give you room to describe the appeal of the item. Why you so desperately wanted it. How you eventually came to obtain it. Why, in some cases, you carted it from place to place throughout your lifetime, even after it was decreed wrong to do so.

No, the form doesn't permit you to say much. Just the facts, please. What is it? Three words or less. Category? Check only one.

Sometimes that's impossible. For example, a chair could be in the category furniture, but it could also be listed under collectibles, or the category, his favourite, or the cat's, or memory. A bed could simply be a piece of furniture, but it rarely is, is it?

Damn bureaucrats and their simple forms. Simple-minded I'd say. No appreciation for history, no sense of love, no awareness of passion. That's for sure.

Dimensions, weight, materials, monetary value, current condition. That's it. Provenance if applicable. How can it not be relevant? There's more to stuff than just the facts, slam, bang, sign the sheet.

Here's my Great Resolve. I will make my own highly personal, totally idiosyncratic list. Each of my treasures, many of which I've hidden away - no, I'm not indicating where they are - may need a few hundred words to describe. Every one will have a story attached to it. A vivid record of the thing and my account of its history and its meaning in my life.

So here I go, Steve. For posterity perhaps? As though the future cares!

No, I'm really doing this for me. I have the storytelling

sting and I must scratch it.

And if you indulge me, Steve, I think that your followers might enjoy hearing the tales of my treasures - many of which will never appear on the official inventory.

Random Notes on *The Decline* - Motor Vehicles

Hello friends, I thought that you might enjoy some offbeat history. Today, Margo Love provides some information about motor vehicles.

Private-use, four-wheeled motor vehicles, also known as automobiles or cars, were the most common form of transportation globally in the 20th and early part of the 21st centuries. Before *The Final Catastrophe,* some 80 million cars were produced worldwide each year with China and the United States of America being the largest markets.

The massive number of cars in operation required the construction of millions of miles of roadways. This necessity led to the intensification of urban sprawl and its concomitant loss of fertile farmland and green space.

Most historians and analysts concur that using private vehicles on such a colossal scale was a primary factor in causing the collapse of civilization.*

Automobiles were powered by gasoline, a volatile fuel and non-renewable resource, that in itself was responsible for such major crimes against humanity as extreme air pollution which led to irreversible global warming; extensive land degradation and depletion of the earth's natural resources; devastating environmental disasters in the world's oceans and inland waterways; and major wars of the late 20th and early 21st centuries.

The vehicles' steel bodies and rubber tires also depleted irreplaceable resources and proved impossible to recycle or to discard safely. The extraction, utilization and disposal of other toxic components such as batteries and exhaust and cooling systems required costly, resource-draining solutions.

During the early years of the 21st century, high fuel prices and concerns about noxious emissions spurred a brief interest in electric vehicles, but these failed to attract consumers on a broad enough scale to make a difference.

The history of automobiles shows a progression from small efficient vehicles like the Volkswagen in the 1930s to ever bigger, uneconomical cars after World War II (1939-1945). This was congruent with the unrestrained expansion of consumerism.

And in the strange history of the rise and fall of motor vehicles, nothing was odder or more disturbing and rarely addressed during their lifespan, than the fact that although almost all automobiles were built with a capacity for four or more passengers, most were only ever used by one person, the driver.

It is estimated that this factor alone led to doubling the number of cars on the road, which indisputably ratcheted up the deleterious effects already noted.

The one driver per automobile norm also exponentially increased not only the number of vehicles that needed to be manufactured, but also the facilities and the space required to store and to park them.

The predictable upsurge in unproductive commuting time and gridlock severely impacted people's health. Although precise statistics are hard to come by, experts conclude that driving cars led to an increase in mortality rates.

This was without taking into account the detrimental

consequences of automobile accidents. Before *The Great Resolve* regulated and severely restricted the use of private vehicles, two million deaths worldwide occurred annually from car accidents.

* see *Private Vehicles Led to The Decline*, K.P. Renaldi; *The Role of Automobiles in Causing The Final Catastrophe*, Jocelyn B. Whitefield; *Cars, the Crime against Civilization and the Monsters who Made Them*, Kevin Maxhead; *Private Vehicles, an Exposé of the World's Most Filthy Habit*, Sam Bjanee; *Automobiles, Automatically Bad*, Mary Lee.

This is only a selection of the more than half a million published documents available online on the role that motor vehicles played in *The Final Catastrophe*. For a full list, go to www.privatevehiclesbigdecline.uew.

Museum of the Obsolete - Fallout Shelters

Hey blog followers, check out the first of some wacky info bits from the past that I'll be posting for your amusement.

The original fallout or bomb shelters were developed during the Cold War (1947-1991) when the imminent threat of nuclear annihilation terrified the world. A look at shelter designs and their recommended survivalist contents provides a thoughtful glimpse into a simple, minimalist lifestyle that we can emulate today.

A resurgence of such shelters took place during *The Decline* when people tried to escape the deadly smog that led to *The Final Catastrophe*. It is not known how many storage lockers were used at that time as pollution-free havens, but estimates suggest that hundreds of thousands of units were inhabited in those dismal years.

The Great Resolve's Un-Paving Paradise initiative razed ancient fallout shelters and all storage facilities to create community gardens.

News Watch

Breaking news from the United Entities of the World: Retired Pope Francis, the 266th leader of the Roman Catholic Church now living on a ranch outside of Buena Vista, was officially declared a saint today - Saint Frank, the first living saint in the Church's history.

In bestowing the honour, Pope Irene Magdalen spoke passionately about how Pope Francis had initiated radical changes to the canon of the tradition-bound Roman Catholic Church during his tenure.

She noted that his alterations have allowed the Church to thrive and grow to become the most popular religion in the world - its three billion followers far surpassing Islam's one billion adherents.

"As Pope, Saint Frank introduced, fast-tracked and implemented such revolutionary modifications to Church doctrine as giving women full equality, lifting the ban on gay and lesbian Catholics having sexual relationships, promoting contraception, making abortion legal for Catholics in any circumstance, and also allowing independent bodies to fully investigate and punish all priests who were suspected and convicted of committing crimes.

"These initiatives made not only the Church but the world a more compassionate environment in which love and peace could flourish," Pope Irene Magdalen said.

"And Saint Frank was a Pope of firsts not only for these accomplishments, but in numerous other unorthodox and ground-breaking ways, both small and momentous."

Saint Frank was the first Pope to embrace a simple lifestyle, choosing to live ascetically. He shunned the papal accommodations offered to him, preferring to sleep in a hostel instead. He ignored private cars to travel aboard buses and carried his own bags when boarding planes.

In fact when he was Pope, Saint Frank totally rejected the sumptuous trappings of his office and the Church hierarchy, ultimately spurning the opulence and enormous wealth of the Vatican itself.

People did not realize back in 2014 when he auctioned off his Harley-Davidson motorcycle to raise money for charity that this was only the start of countless enterprises that would directly lead to the most radical undertaking in the history of the Catholic Church.

This was, of course, the wholesale dissolution of the vast holdings of the Vatican and the re-distribution of its colossal assets (estimated at $200 billion) to the needy and homeless all around the world. In fact, this achievement became his legacy and what many believe led to his sainthood today.

Pope Francis walked the talk of simple living before it was fashionable to do so. And his example enabled the surprisingly easy transition of what had been a medieval anachronistic institution into a showpiece of philanthropy in the 21st century.

As a key forerunner to *The Great Resolve*, Pope Francis lived *The Naked Law* before it existed. His unconventional practices were evident from the beginning.

Just after becoming Pope, he marked Holy Thursday by washing the feet of two female prisoners at a detention centre for young offenders. Women had never before been included in this sacred Easter-time ritual that recalled Jesus washing the feet of his disciples.

Pope Irene Magdalen noted that Saint Frank was a papal pioneer in tapping the electronic media to collect feedback from Catholics worldwide, and then using the information gathered from the people themselves to make numerous historic changes.

He was also the very first Pope to take a selfie and to use Twitter. The photo of the then 76-year-old Pope posing with teenagers in 2013 and his remark for them "to make noise" went viral across social media at the time.

The reaction of Catholics and non-Catholics around the globe to his sainthood was highly emotional and almost universally positive.

The Seven Crimes of Consumerism

Over the next few blogs, In the Middle of Things brings you instalments of Controller Elliott Rampart's Keynote Address at the Annual Conference of Global Government Advisors. Here's his intro:

Thank you for inviting me to speak this evening at your annual conference. I am honoured to participate in such a worthy congress and bring greetings from my colleagues at the United Entities of the World.

And before I begin, on behalf of the UEW, I would like to acknowledge and commend you for taking time out of your demanding schedules to not only listen to my address, broadcast live here in beautiful Arcadia and distributed virtually through the All Point Teleconferencing System, but also to take part in what must be one of the most significant forums in the world today.

I can assure you that the discussions and reports that you will be monitoring, debating and analysing during your three-day meeting will have a monumental impact.

The outcomes of this gathering will help determine the decisions, policies and procedures of local governments worldwide. These results will have a profound influence on global institutions and corporations, and most importantly, on the lives of every citizen in the world today, and those yet to be born.

I feel deeply privileged to be standing before you. I hope my presentation will not only be relevant to the proceedings, but that it will encourage you in your valuable work.

In tonight's talk, I will first outline and provide some background information about our fundamental document, *The Seven Crimes of Consumerism*. The SCC was one of the primary tenets issued after *The Great Resolve.* It led to most, if not all, of the 1,666 laws endorsed by the UEW.

As those of you here know, *The Great Resolve* that resulted in the development of *The Naked Law* was brought about by a proliferation of overconsumption and a glut of materialism on a scale so vast that it threatened to destroy our planet.

Let me start by giving you just one shocking statistic that illustrates the sick society of *The Decline* era. As early as 2011, Consumerites were spending $1.2 trillion a year, ten percent of total annual purchases, on things that they didn't need. That's $1.2 trillion on completely unnecessary stuff. Unconscionable indeed!

During *The Great Resolve* seven crimes were identified as leading to the near collapse of civilization. These were: Envy, Gluttony, Greed, Lust, Pride, Sloth, and Wrath.

As an historical aside, it may interest you to realize that

these same seven wrongs have been recognized since early Christian times, long before *The Final Catastrophe*, under their ancient religious name: *The Seven Deadly Sins*.

The Catholic Church regarded them as cardinal sins, the most vile of all vices that if practised and not confessed could lead to eternal damnation. And beginning in the early 14th century, European artists used *The Seven Deadly Sins* as a theme in their art in order to educate people and ingrain these grievous faults in their consciousness.

Obviously, as evidenced by *The Decline* and *The Final Catastrophe*, the religious propaganda failed to have any effect on the populace and these sins continued to flourish into the 21st century.

In this presentation, I will give you an in-depth review of each of the seven crimes of consumerism, one by one.

I will systematically identify what each misdeed means not just legally as outlined in the laws prohibiting them, but also psychologically as described in the latest edition of the Diagnostic and Statistical Manual of Mental Disorders and realistically as practised by criminals.

As well, I will provide one momentous example of a product that encapsulated the very essence of these seven offences against humanity. This was an item so ubiquitous during *The Decline* that many people believe that it alone led to *The Final Catastrophe*.

I will demonstrate, in my remarks, how this at one time progressive and innovative product not only outlived its usefulness, but caused disastrous damage worldwide on a scale so massive as to be thought implausible if only it were not, sadly, fact.

To wrap up, I will give you details about what the UEW is doing to ensure that these violations are held in check and that those who flout the law are swiftly caught and severely punished. Then I expect that we will have a few minutes for questions and for sharing how your administrations are implementing the laws and dealing with the miscreants.

Qs & As from the Clutter-Buster's Blog

Dear Clutter-Buster:

I was raised to believe that if you brought something into your home, you must take something out. My husband of forty years has suddenly decided differently.

He recently bought a pair of new shoes which he badly needed as his old ones were worn on the soles and had holes in the leather uppers.

An independent shoe appraiser signed the form allowing for the purchase of replacement footwear. However, my husband refuses to dispose of the old pair. When I asked why he didn't just hand them over when he bought the new shoes, which by law he is supposed to do, he said he forgot.

Then I found out that he had told the young clerk that he had an exemption to keep the old pair for gardening.

We do not have a garden. Do you think this could be a sign of Alzheimer's? What do I do? - *in for the long haul*

Dear In for the Long Haul:

Refusing to get rid of useless things was one of the major factors that ultimately led to *The Final Catastrophe*. It's why de-cluttering laws were urgently required to save our world. But rules only work if people obey them.

Some individuals do have a hard time parting with stuff that they've grown accustomed to. I fear that your husband is one of those, at least as far as his shoes are concerned.

A little compassion on your part is OK, but so is some tough-love vigilance. The inability to discard worthless items could be one sign, not necessarily of Alzheimer's, but of a hoarding compulsion. If not nipped in the bud, it could lead to full scale addiction and more irrational behaviour.

You may want to have a look in your husband's dresser drawers to see if he has kept other worn-out stuff.

If he has, then you have a problem that needs to be dealt with promptly by medical professionals who are experienced with treating mentally ill people.

Sheri Does the Inventory Her Way!

Let me begin with one of the first things that I lusted over. And then you tell me in which category it belongs on the idiotic Essential Goods Inventory form.

It was in that most joyous of times at the outset of my marriage. My husband and I had been in the habit of frequenting used goods stores which, I must clarify, were not like our current sterile and utilitarian disposal facilities.

These shops accepted donations from people who no longer needed some of their possessions. Their cast-offs ranged from jewellery to musical instruments, clothing to furniture, appliances to toys, decorative pieces to utensils and tools. Virtually everything that anyone owned could be found neatly arranged in these outlets.

The goods, while second-hand (I always thought that was part of their charm), were in fine shape, repaired and cleaned as required. And not only students shopped there and not just poor people either.

To some of us, these early haunts remained a part of our lives throughout the years, even after we could afford to buy new at brand name emporiums. So you can well imagine what a predicament it was during *The Decline* when the government closed them down. But that's another story.

While we were consumers, I dare say that we were in the forefront of the anti-consumer society, although that has now been forgotten. After all, we bought and used and valued things that, if it weren't for us, would have been destined for the dump, adding to the huge garbage disposal problem that unquestionably contributed to *The Decline*.

Anyway, while browsing in one of our favourite stores, we came across a pair of old string wicker chairs.

They were made over a century ago and had been initially sold through a catalogue. That's a paper book illustrating a wide variety of products for sale. It allowed people to buy merchandise even if they couldn't go to an actual store.

Now that I think of it, these mail order catalogues were much like shopping online. Once an order was placed, it was delivered right to the door. At that time by horse and buggy rather than by drones.

String wicker was in style back in Victorian times and although out of fashion when we discovered them, we found these handsome, oversized chairs immensely appealing.

One was a rocker, and both had thick back and seat cushions stuffed with horse-hair. They were upholstered in dark brown velvet that, I will concede, was quite threadbare in spots.

For years, these two well-made antiques served as the most comfortable seats in the flats that we lived in.

They came though with a peculiar history. When we first spied them, they sported a hand-scrawled "Hold" sign. The clerk assured us that they were still for sale. An earlier customer did not have enough money and had asked that they be kept until he could pay for them. The store agreed to hold them until he returned with the payment, unless someone else wanted to buy them in the meantime.

We paid for the chairs and only when they were delivered with the hold tags still on, did we notice that they had been reserved by someone we knew. I felt badly for his loss, but at the same time gloated over our gain.

I never did tell him about our find and years later when I heard about his suicide, I felt horribly guilty about the way that we had acquired the chairs, literally pulling them out from under him.

It was then after more than a decade of comfort and joy that I could no longer sit on them. Even just seeing them in our living room caused me to break down in tears. I wondered irrationally if their loss had contributed to his demise. So I relegated them to the basement where they still sit as I write their topsy-turvy history.

By that time the chairs had been repaired. Over the years, the heat in our apartments and houses had dried out the wicker and our cats sharpening their claws on them caused many breaks in the weave.

Let me tell you, it was an adventure in itself getting them fixed as few craftspeople were familiar with deteriorating natural fibres. But my father, a carpenter, had started a network of artisans. He located a couple in a village up north who made beautiful willow and rush furniture and they were able to fix our dilapidated pieces.

Once that was done, I had the natural horse-hair in the cushions replaced with synthetic foam and reupholstered in sumptuous British-made Sanderson fabric.

I regret doing this now. How it hurts to have destroyed something authentically old. But at the time, the whole acquisition of this expensive upholstery had filled me with a sense of glee at having succeeded professionally enough to be able to afford such luxury.

Needless to say, it was a purchase way out of my league. I was raised in a working class family where I sought out remnants on sale and sewed my own clothes. But I can remember impressing a number of people when I mentioned Sanderson. Oh my, how my insecurity embarrasses me now.

A Chorus of Voices - Come Purge with Us

You're invited to the 10th annual Solstice Purge Parade and Bonfire to celebrate nothingness.

Here's your chance to take part in a neighbourhood event, have some fun and do good at the same time.

You know the mantra: *I have enough, I do enough, I am enough.* Chant it loudly and chant it proudly as you march in the Giant Purge Parade and join in the Massive Clear-Out and Bonfire at the Ridit Rink and Skating Park.

Get rid of your stuff in a safe, secure and festive way.

To make the most of this special occasion, don't just bring things you can do without, no longer use, are tired of, or that your kids have outgrown.

Push yourself beyond the limits and bring goods that you truly love and those that you feel you couldn't possibly live without. Things that fit on your inventory. Items that you are allowed to keep. Objects that you cherish.

Take up the challenge to get rid of your possessions. You will feel so cleansed after the Purge.

Remember that items you bring must be non-toxic when burned. No more than ten articles per family. Register today.

Sponsored by your local Buy Nothing Committee.

Laszlo the Fixer

Today on my blog, I want to introduce you to Laszlo Lorca, a rebel with a cause and one of a dying breed.

No pun intended, but Laszlo is undeniably dying as we all are every day of our lives. Laszlo though may be closer to the end than most of us because of his age. But no one knows when any of us will "shuffle off this mortal coil," so perhaps at 95 years young, he may well outlive us all.

And more power to him if he does as he's had a hard life, although you'd never guess it to look at him now.

During The Decline, Laszlo was part of an infamous band of renegades - hard-working artisans of lost arts who specialized in repairing old and broken things. The Fixers, as they called themselves, had expertise in many ancient crafts and trades and they were professional restorers.

They were, however, looked down upon as little better than wandering gypsies or homeless vagrants.

What was their crime?

Admittedly, it wasn't actually a punishable offence. It was more of an affront to the upright residents of the Kingdom of Consumer Land.

Those citizens shunned the Fixers as though they were members of a secret society or cult. While acknowledging their useful skills, the Consumerites despised the Fixers' apparent contentment and their ability to live and to thrive within their means.

Their very existence made a mockery of those slaves to work and overconsumption, and to all that the decadent culture before The Final Catastrophe espoused.

Thank you, Laszlo, for being able to share your time live with my blog followers.

Let me kick off this interview with some basic questions about your life as a member of the Fixers' collective and then we'll move on to some of the broader details about your philosophy and your influences.

First, can you tell me a bit about yourself and how you came to be a Fixer?

Well Steve, you know the old saw "one door closes and another opens." That's exactly what happened to me, although I didn't see it as an opportunity at the time.

For a short while after getting my papers as a master carpenter, I worked for a firm constructing houses in new subdivisions. It was, in fact, the same company where I had apprenticed while in school.

Then low-cost, pre-fab houses that required no trained workers at all took the market by storm and I was suddenly out of work.

These cookie-cutter dwellings came in Ikea-like kits with easy-to-follow instructions. Anyone with Lego experience could put these places together in three or four days.

No kidding, if you played with blocks as a kid, you could build your own house. That's how these structures were marketed and they sold like umbrellas during a rainstorm.

After being unemployed for several years, I found work at a furniture company.

It didn't really make good use of my expertise, but it was a job of sorts and I desperately needed the money as by then I had two daughters.

At that time though, manufacturing businesses across the continent were shutting down like dominoes, one right after another. They couldn't compete with the cheap labour in

Third World countries.

This was the new norm during *The Decline*. And sure enough a few years later, the furniture company laid me off and filed for bankruptcy.

To tell you the truth, neither of those jobs was especially fulfilling. When I was unemployed though, I helped my friends and relatives by repairing things - a broken chair, a warped drawer, a cabinet door.

They paid me a little and I felt good making some old thing work again. It kept the items from being thrown out and I quite liked handling vintage pieces. I could appreciate their craftsmanship.

And I felt as if I was carrying on a tradition by saving the handiwork of wood-workers from bygone eras.

I liked using my carpentry skills to make new things, too - like when my sister had her first child, I made a beautiful arts and crafts style rocking cradle. So I became an expert fixer of wooden items, and a maker as well.

During that time I was also hawking my handicrafts at local fairs. Mostly small pieces - birdhouses, walking sticks, duck decoys, boxes - that kind of thing.

Plus, I took on commissioned jobs. There was always someone who wanted a special gift made from wood.

And with the advent of the Internet, I was able to sell more broadly. I created a website and had a nice little enterprise. I called it *Out of the Woods*.

You seem to have a special relationship with wood? How did that come about?

The roots of my passion run deep. I remember playing a lot with twigs and branches as a kid. Even as a toddler, I would stack the firewood that my dad had chopped into neat bundles by the cottage door.

When I got older, I liked having the job of carrying logs inside, throwing them into the fireplace and watching them burn. I recall being mesmerized by the mysterious shapes rising out of the flames and then collapsing and turning to powdery ash.

I have fond memories of walking in the forest at the cottage or in the ravine near our home and collecting fallen tree boughs.

I had a pen knife and used it to turn long firm sticks into spears and smaller pieces into daggers. I particularly loved the smell of fresh wood and nothing gave me more pleasure than to see the shavings pile up as I whittled away.

For one Mother's Day when I was about seven, I carved my mom a beautiful life-size robin which she kept on her bedside table all her long life.

In grade school I made my first box. It was a simple rough-hewn thing, but I remember that I gave it proudly to my dad for his birthday.

I loved everything about working with wood, and still do.

I guess I was a born tree-hugger, too - appreciating trees in all seasons: quietly budding in the spring, sporting their luxurious green foliage at the peak of summer, showing off their glory in a blaze of autumn colours, and looking solemn and peaceful, bare-branched in the pure white snow.

Trekking along the Bruce Trail became a lifelong passion starting when I was in my teens and joined a hiking club at school. And entrance points to footpaths always lay close to wherever I lived.

So you can see how it came about that I grew to be a wood-worker.

Museum of the Obsolete - Phone Booths

A phone booth contained a telephone that anyone could pay to activate. People wanting to talk to someone would deposit coins or insert credit cards in a slot on the phone apparatus and then proceed to make a call.

The small enclosed structure was made of plastic and metal to withstand heavy use and external elements.

It usually had lighting, a door to provide privacy, and windows to let others know if the phone was being used. Some booths contained a printed directory of local telephone numbers and a seat.

In the early part of the 20th century and continuing up in to the 1990s, these cubicles were a universal feature of the urban landscape and also part of popular culture.

They were most commonly located outside, every few blocks on city streets and in central locations such as beside a general store or a restaurant in small towns. Some were also placed indoors in hospitals, hotels, restaurants, train depots, bus stations and airports.

In the fiction of that time, the comic-book superhero Superman was said to have used these booths to quickly shed his work-a-day suit and change into his iconic crime-fighting uniform. Doctor Who's blue British police call box travelled through space and time, and Maxwell Smart's stall gave him access to the hidden headquarters of CONTROL.

By the late 20th century however, most phone booths had been replaced by non-enclosed pay phones or kiosks.

This increased their accessibility for disabled people and discouraged lengthy calls in high-demand areas.

During *The Decline,* the rise of mobile phones resulted in the extinction of all public pay phones.

Qs & As from the Clutter-Buster's Blog

Dear Clutter-Buster:

I've recently noticed a strange activity on the part of my neighbour of many years. In the very early hours while it is still dark and before dog-walkers are out and about, I have seen her carrying a small flash-light and digging rather large holes in her backyard. She seems to dig deeply and looks around furtively as she is doing this.

I haven't seen her place anything in the holes yet, but I wonder if she is going to be hiding things there. Right now she just covers them up again with stones.

What should I do? - *nervous neighbour*

Dear Nervous Neighbour:

This behaviour does appear quite bizarre. But as there is no law preventing people from digging holes on their property, I do not think you have to be alarmed. And you have no need to report her actions to the authorities unless you have concrete evidence that she is burying illegal items.

I do wonder though about you. Why are you awake at such odd hours seemingly with nothing else to do except peer into the darkness, watching your neighbour? It seems a bit obsessive and voyeuristic on your part. You might want to check out sleep and anxiety disorders with your doctor.

The Seven Crimes of Consumerism

Fellow Global Government Advisors, let me begin my talk with the crime of Envy. Being jealous and hating people for what they have - their possessions.

As hard as it is to believe nowadays, before *The Great Resolve* this offence was not only widespread, but also greatly celebrated.

Slick advertising and incessant marketing messages on every device and communications network, along with the overt media saturation of celebrity endorsements, infused masses of people with spiteful Envy.

This ruinous characteristic caused a huge number of the populace to get more and more in debt buying things that they did not need and could ill afford.

Indeed, financial difficulties were frequently so acute that innumerable folk could not cope. They went bankrupt, losing their self-respect, as well as their homes and families in a dastardly downhill slide.

All because of unrestrained covetousness.

In its most extreme form, a jealous person is someone who not only thinks they should have more of what others have, but who also wants to deprive others of their things.

So what starts out as a personal obsession often becomes an evil trait that affects countless innocent acquaintances of the offender.

And a mind poisoned with invidious resentment can all too easily embrace such misdeeds as lying and stealing.

Psychologists, psychiatrists, medical doctors and social workers are obligated by law to report patients who exhibit the mental torment associated with Envy.

Unfortunately, as you all know only too well, by the time this malicious criminality is brought to court, it will already have caused suffering to everyone who has come in contact with the perpetrator.

So catching the wrong-doing before it has progressed is imperative in order to curtail its impact on society.

Today, thanks to *The Naked Law*, *The Grand Inventory* and the banning of advertising, we are happily seeing fewer cases of this violation. And those that do come before the courts are being severely dealt with.

Mandatory depossessioning and solitary confinement are two of the most commonly imposed punishments.

Sheri Does the Inventory Her Way!

Chairs have played a large role in my life as they have in most people's, if they'd only stop and think about it.

Consider that even this highly limiting inventory form that I have to fill out allows for six chairs per person which is actually quite a few for each individual.

How many do you really need?

A sturdy stool to perch on while eating, a cushiony one for relaxing in, an ergonomically precise computer chair, perhaps another task chair for your hobby or recreational use, and a couple for company.

There you have it. Inventory complete.

But what do you do about the furniture that you need for sitting outside on your balcony, patio or deck?

The collapsible chair that you take to the beach, and to the park for concerts? The sturdy oak one that serves as a step ladder when you need to climb up to get something from the high cupboards? The bench near the front door where your park yourself to put on your shoes or boots?

The chintz wing chair positioned by the window, so you can watch the birds come to the feeder or the neighbours puttering around in their gardens?

What about an extra chair to put your feet on since the form leaves no room for footstools?

I must confess that before *The Great Resolve* and *The Grand Inventory*, I collected (*mea culpa*) lots of chairs in addition to the two wicker ones that I've just told you about.

Another memorable one was an ornately carved, red leather chaise longue with an accompanying throne chair that I was told came from a captain's quarters on a ship.

We bought these magnificent pieces at a swanky shop in Cabbagetown, a part of Toronto known at the time for its antique and decor stores. They were not cheap, but we were working then, and therefore able to pay for this, our first major household purchase, with our savings.

I remember the cool autumnal day when we first spotted the chaise in the window. We didn't know when we saw it that there was an accompanying chair.

Oh my, the chaise yes, but what would we do with the throne? The proprietor was adamant - the two could not be parted. Take both or none.

We conceded and brought the behemoths into our small worker's cottage. They filled our entire living room.

But they filled it beautifully, and really, what more did two people newly in love need?

The room truly became our intimate lounge for relaxing and we relished sitting there together after long days at work. And my, how one could unwind, sprawled on the chaise, sipping Mimosas and nibbling chocolates while looking through the Sunday papers.

This was long ago, and I must say, it's just not the same reading the news on a tab. Part of the sheer decadence of the old days was sharing the newspaper sections with your lover and dropping them on the floor as you finished each part.

I know that this is hard to explain to a younger generation raised without newspapers and printed magazines, but for us old folk this experience was pure bliss. And it made for a perfectly lazy Sunday morning.

Part of the appeal of these antiquities was their history, not just the details of their construction. I wondered who had carved the solid oak into figureheads, scrollwork, cabriole legs and claw feet, and who had made the solid brass tacks and fitted them meticulously into the rich red leather.

But even more fascinating to me was the mystery of all those who had owned and sat upon the chaise longue and throne since they were built in the late 19th century.

The chaise was meant for taking it easy, so I can't help but imagine what daydreams and dalliances were part of her background. I say her intentionally as I'm unable to envision this type of chair as masculine.

I picture the patients of an esteemed doctor of psychiatry such as Dr. Freud or Dr. Jung, reclining on just such a divan. The delicate invalid would most likely have been female, or perhaps a frail man.

I see the psychiatrist, always robustly male in my mind, perched rigidly on the sturdy, hard-backed throne which is positioned slightly behind the chaise longue.

The revered doctor is, of course, well-groomed, wearing a tweed suit and sporting a beard that he strokes occasionally as he listens to his patient's outpourings of woe. His hand holds a gold Waterman fountain pen, and on his lap lies an open Moleskine notebook.

And I do picture the throne as masculine too, despite such throne-sitters as the queens, Victoria and the two Elizabeths.

My stereotypes, my imagination or lack thereof!

What incredible stories these pieces of furniture have been privy to over the many years of their existence. If only they could speak.

A Chorus of Voices - Jamie Confesses

Hello blogsters, I just wanted to let you know what this posting is all about.

As part of his rehab treatment, Jamie is making his confession public by way of In the Middle of Things.

I remember my granma. She was so ahead of her time. A real stickler for recycling - way back before the law.

Hard to believe now with the Magic Nine on every block that there was a time when people put stuff that they no longer wanted in garbage bags and set them out for the authorities to get rid of.

Gran said that workers drove their pollution-spouting mega-trucks slowly up and down the streets picking up bag after bag of trash.

Stop, pick up, toss, compact, inch along to the next few houses. Stop, pick up, toss, compact, over and over again.

Where were the robos? And really, having someone else get rid of your stuff, yuck!

People back then sure were inconsideros.

Yahoo! I love it mucho when my apparat lights up with the Primary: *Naked you came into this world, naked you must leave it.*

It isn't every time you get that mem as your screensave. It feels like I won the lott. A little perk to start my day. Hooray!

My gran told me about *The Great Resolve* and how the Controllers decided against implanting the new laws in your brain, or hiding them in sublim messages like they did with adverts in PC days.

She said there was a year-long conflab - back and forth,

pros and cons - until they finally opted for straight-on clearspeak. Concise. To the point. No need for high-priced legal-beagles to decode the laws. No hidden meanings to decipher and interpret. Not in the nova.

And personally, I think that's good. Gran did, too. What could be easier - you turn on your tool, hit home and there it is: so simply awesome - *The Naked Law*.

But gran said that at the time citizens rallied against the plain talk of the law.

And they weren't all just legals or those who could make moola from gobblegook like govie bureaucrackpots.

No, they were just ordinaries who liked upmarket words and thought that the laws were dumbed down to the lowest, and that we would lose so much poetry lingo.

Gimme a break!

Gran said that debates raged on and on, pitting Mr. Spock and the Rationalites against Captain Kirk and his Poetics. She sided with the Spockites as did most of the Controllers. But rational common sense ruled; naked language got norm.

I think that people instinctively know what's best. You don't have to whack them with it, do you? Gran summed it up in four words: "Keep it simple, stupid!"

Oh lookie, now I got one of the Mighty Maxs in view: *If you bring something in, take something out.*

Pretty basic, right? No need for interpros. You want that doggie in the window. Well, get rid of the mutt you have.

No, you can't just get another and add to your menagerie. Who do you think you are, Emily Carr for cripes sake? And no, it doesn't matter if you can afford it or not.

Gran said that in those days the people who could least pay for things were often the most materialistic. Crazee!

But apparently they were encouraged by massive, and

I mean colosso, in-your-face, and hidden, adverts.

She said it was Consumerites who rented all the storage lockers that totally ate up the fertile farm land. Man, they often spent more on storing things that they didn't use than they paid for rent.

And gran wasn't simply making up stories. I saw snips on Life Groove about peeps back then and it was so black bad, I needed a bang afterwards to just go on. Sicko, eh?

Gran said hoarding got added to the DSM after those real TV shows in the early 21st made fun of obsessy-collectos. That's when de-cluttering became a profession and you needed a psych degree before you could get your pro-des.

Gran said that as soon as accumulators were designated certifiably mentally ill, you couldn't stop the raging growth of De-Clutterers Anon and all the other self-helps - Secret Over-Users, Waste-Watchers, Hoarders Be Gone, Everyday Extenders, Encumbered No More, Clutter-Away, Muddlers, The Mess-Ups.

She would be surprised though to learn that De-Clutterers Anon is still booming. No crappo, it's the biggest selfie-orgo in the world.

That's because hoarding stuff is wild and even after the Final, there are millions of thing-addicts around. Not just from her generation, but from peeps born after the FC.

Dudes like me.

And I'm so friggin' glad she doesn't know that I'm one of the collecto junkies, and a totally sorry member of DCA.

With all the stories that my gran told me when I was little, I honestly can't say how I ended up this way.

Freaky synchro, eh?

I know mom and dad had a tough time following the new laws at first. They weren't compulsive-collectos or OTT, just typicals born BTD and influenced early on by the media into buying more than they could use.

In fact, even before *The Decline,* mom would, every once in a while, embark on a purge - doing what she called spring cleaning. And dad would have a garage clear-out, back when it was still legal.

So I don't think that it was genetic or even shaped by my enviro. I just sort of fell into it, I guess.

Peer pressure? Yeah, well maybe.

Like I didn't know Tom was HA till long after he joined DCA, even though there were signs early on.

I discovered his pen obsess when I saw him sitting under a tree in the park fidgeting with this sharp silver thing on what I later learned was a book made of paper.

He flushed and started stuttering when he saw that I'd seen him and begged me not to blab. He swore that he didn't do it often, but sometimes he just couldn't stop himself. He found that writing with a pen on paper helped him calm.

Poor sod, he couldn't get his Zen just stroking his tab.

He let me hold the pen and write in his book. I found it hard to wrap my fingers around the cold stylus, and pressing down on the soft paper felt weird and hurt my finger-tips and knuckles.

Tom told me that if I didn't snitch, he would let me do it again.

Big whoop! To tell you true, it frankly didn't grab my endorphs. But I let him think that it did.

I forgot about Tom's HA until Samantha, who I was serio over, told me that she would never get rid of her rings, no matter what the law said. Rings from her grans and aunties that had been saved during *The General Meltdown.*

No, she wasn't wearing them. I discovered her stash

when I began sleeping over.

Her family had, sure enough, boarded up all closets when *The No Closet Law* came into effect, so she had nowhere to hide her rings. She kept them wrapped in a carved wooden box on her bedside table.

The box was verboten under *The Banning of All Storage Containers Act.*

But hey, you gotta have a bit of proho, don't you?

I noticed the box right away although it was days before she let me see what was in it.

What could I say?

She never wore the rings, so I didn't think that this was way wacko bad. What harm in a few glitzy trinks?

Sammie just wanted to keep some things from her fam. And it's not like she went out and added to her collection - not that I know of anyway.

I kinda lusted after the box though. It seemed like such a wonderway to store (whoops, I didn't mean to swear) treasures (whoops again) in.

I know, I know, the wood that went into the box and Tom's book and the metal that went into the rings and the pens used up Mama Nat's bounty, and this was bad.

Still, since you asked, I guess that Tom's and Sammie's has-to-havos might have influenced me. And I admit that I kinda craved after something bizarro of my own.

I guess I thought that because I hid my stuff, it wouldn't matter. Nobody would find out. But I now recognize how wrong I was, and how damn tricky it is to stop a habo.

When they took my things away, I didn't know what to do. So I just slept a lot and played ringo way-obsesso until my thumbs cracked. They told me that I had to join DCA and make a public confession. So here it is.

Museum of the Obsolete - Lawns

In the 20th century vast swaths of invaluable land were cultivated with grass, short green plants with long narrow leaves. These highly desirable areas around houses, golf courses and parks were known as lawns.

Appallingly, this vegetation required copious amounts of priceless water and regular infusions of toxic chemicals to survive. And to maintain their tidy appearance, lawns also needed to be meticulously and regularly groomed.

Mechanical machines, known as lawn mowers, used revolving blades to cut the grass. The blades were mostly powered by electricity or by gas. Riding mowers were used for large expanses.

During *The Decline,* automated robotic mowers became standard for trimming this vegetation.

Laws enacted after *The Great Resolve* banned grasslands because of their detrimental environmental impact and the unwarranted waste of resources necessary to sustain them. This effectively eliminated the need for lawn mowers and they also became obsolete.

Qs & As from the Clutter-Buster's Blog

Dear Clutter-Buster:

My days on this lovely planet are limited as recently I was diagnosed with a fatal disease.

I know that I should be filling out all the government forms that go with the end of life and the final disposal of worldly goods. But I don't want to spend my precious remaining days doing this. Is it unethical not to bother?

I have no family who would have to deal with the fallout from my actions after my death. Only the paid bureaucrats will. - *wanting to play*

Dear Wanting to Play:

Please accept my sincere condolences. My heart goes out to you and your quandary. I would like to say enjoy your remaining time and do only things that leave you feeling good. But I would be remiss if I advised you to do that.

Although you may feel as if you are completely alone with your prognosis, you are not. In reality, thousands of people receive such dire news daily.

And statistics show that about 150,000 people die every single day. Many of these deaths are not accidental, so, like you, they knew their prospects beforehand.

You must also consider the severe strain on government systems if all the people who had terminal illnesses were to disobey *The End of Life Law*.

This decree was put in place to help everyone still alive after your passing, and the generations yet to come.

It would be immoral for me to tell you to follow your bliss and ignore the law.

You must, in good conscience, fill out the forms to the best of your ability, and the sooner the better.

Laszlo the Fixer

How did the collective come about?

Well Steve, if you were a carpenter, but not a Jack or Jill of all trades, you sometimes needed to find someone who could repair things for you. And it's kind of inbred in most people who work with their hands that stuff shouldn't just be thrown out and replaced with new items, but should, if possible, be fixed.

So for instance, when a couple of pieces of a stained glass window, which my wife valued, broke, I asked if anyone knew any glaziers. And not surprisingly, they did.

I added the names to my growing list of contacts and later if one of my customers needed glass restored, I could hook them up.

I'll give you another example. My daughter had these dilapidated, antique wicker chairs. She couldn't find anyone locally who could refurbish them.

I asked around and found in a little town not too far away, a couple who made fine willow furniture and they restored the chairs for her.

And that's how it started. I soon had lists of artisans for every sort of thing - a guy who got cell phones back in working order, a woman who renewed mechanical clocks, a young man who not only sharpened knives, but could patch up all sorts of metal objects, and a leather crafter who mended shoes, boots, belts and purses.

You could usually find someone, often in your own neighbourhood, who could overhaul anything. So you can see that a whole community was growing.

It was also part of the do-it-yourself trend that happened in the first years of the Millennium.

And by then, needless to say, if you couldn't locate Fixers by word of mouth, you just had to go online and Google. That's how I discovered a specialist who could recondition some antique frames that I had.

In fact, there was a whole network of industrious craftspeople everywhere, and also the greatest educational device ever - YouTube. And Fixers were right in there from the start making how-to videos and posting them online.

That is what I think is way cool about Fixers - we want to help. We like sharing.

To my mind, that's really quite a splendid way of living.

The Seven Crimes of Consumerism

My esteemed colleagues, let me move on now to Gluttony, the second crime of consumerism.

The ancient Italian poet Dante called this the sin of excessive pleasure.

However, I find it hard to believe that there could be any enjoyment connected with this irresponsible and selfish misconduct. Indeed, the overconsumption of food and drink is more than anything an offence against one's body caused by one's mind.

Immoderate eating and drinking ultimately leads to the wanton destruction of one's physical being, inside and out, through all sorts of dastardly illnesses and crippling disabilities such as obesity, diabetes, heart disease and alcoholism, to name just a few.

One must not forget that the root of this self-destructive behaviour lies in mental illness.

And overusing food and drink in an attempt to satisfy one's relentless cravings and to escape one's psychological demons leads to dreadful obsessive-compulsive habits, addictions, depression and social isolation.

Deplorably, this misdeed, like most crimes, all too soon expands to seriously affect others - most notably, relatives, friends and co-workers. Gluttony is implicated in such transgressions as stealing, wasting food, and not giving food to the needy. And obviously, it has a costly and detrimental impact on the health care system.

That's why the law mandates that not only medical workers, but anyone aware of people in the grip of Gluttony must report these miscreants to the Department of Health and Well-Being.

Only then can this crime be curtailed.

Fortunately, *The Tracking of Consumables Act* enables us to identify, apprehend and monitor gluttonous lawbreakers more effectively.

And for convicted felons, sentences commonly include mandatory rehab treatment in certified programs of such global organizations as Overeaters No More, Food Addicts Inc, Gluttony Unbound, Alco-Anon and Sober Up.

Only when these remedies fail do we initiate highly successful medical interventions such as bariatric surgery and electroconvulsive therapy.

Sheri Does the Inventory Her Way!

It has always puzzled me how getting one treasure somehow breeds a yearning for another. And I suppose that even such a mild obsession spread over millions of people was not sustainable, and our get-more compulsions ultimately led to *The Final Catastrophe*.

We know this now, but back then my husband and I were just starting out on the adventure of our lives and that trip included the gathering of possessions. Many were utilitarian and now long gone, broken down and disposed of.

I will not go into those things here. They don't belong in my personal inventory although, in some cases, traces of their existence still surface from time to time. It doesn't take much to set memories in motion.

So no stories, for example, about the mahogany dining room table and chairs passed down through generations from my great-grandparents to end up with me.

I won't tell you about the time when I was a child, probably four or five years old, visiting my grandparents who then owned this particular suite. For some silly reason, I shoved my head between the back uprights and the vase-shaped splats of one of the chairs.

I must have had a unique view of the hardwood and Indian rug on the floor. However, when it was time to move, I could not extricate my head from the chair. The more I tried, the more I cried and the more my head was stuck.

Mama came running to see what the fuss was and I believe now that she must have stifled a laugh as she tried to calm me down and help me out of my predicament.

But she couldn't, and I continued to sob as she left to get my grandfather. He took one look at the sad spectacle of his grandchild caught like a prisoner in the stockades and went to his workshop in the basement to get a saw.

I wailed even more at the thought that he was going to cut off my head. But, needless to say, he didn't and I was soon released from my self-made trap.

Whenever I dusted the dining room suite that this chair belonged to, I remembered not only my misadventure, but also my mother and my grandfather, both long gone.

And I took extra care to tenderly polish the chair of my childish folly. I knew which one it was because grandpa had repaired it with a splat that didn't quite match.

I never stuck my head into the back of a chair again. I was reluctant to don a bicycle helmet, and I was terrified in later years when I had to position my head in an MRI device.

A frisson of fear would also flash through me every time our cats crawled into the narrow spaces beneath a sideboard or under a counter.

But unlike me whose terror of being trapped surely made my head swell until it totally filled the hole that I had got myself into, my graceful felines were always able to shimmy their way out.

That nonsense makes me recall the drop-leaf table that we carted from home to new home over the course of thirty-five years. It came from my grandfather's workshop, the same place where he went to get his saw.

When my parents disposed of his things after he died, I took the table. Its surface was stained and marked, but its legs were sturdy.

I remember painting it peacock blue, my favourite colour, and using it in our kitchen for years. All through the time of our children's growing up. So many family dinners and birthday cakes shared around that old table.

It had one drawer that became a hidey-hole for little findings - pebbles, chestnuts, shells, acorns, ginkgo leaves - that the kids had discovered, or that I had picked up on my early morning walks.

Eventually, the table became rickety and it was relegated to the garage where dampness took its toll. And overloaded with heavy storage boxes, my lovely table finally collapsed under the burden.

I managed to salvage the drawer and the legs before the rest of the table was unceremoniously tossed.

I created a *memento mori* in the drawer and hung it on the wall in the family room.

And whenever I'm on the back deck, I see the well-turned table legs thrusting their optimistic blue skywards from the backyard fern garden where I had planted them. So blatantly cheery. So awfully sad.

Oh Steve, I need a break. My emotional attachment to things disturbs me.

Museum of the Obsolete - Wrist Watches

Throughout the 20th century, people encircled their wrists with bands of metal, leather or plastic that had miniature time-telling mechanisms attached to them.

Prior to the invention of these wrist watches in the 1920s, similar timepieces had been attached to a chain and worn around the neck or carried in a pocket.

The advent of cell phones made one-use, time-keeping mechanisms anachronistic.

During *The Decline,* wrist watches were worn mainly as fashion statements or status symbols. And paradoxically, the labour intensive, intricate and aesthetic workmanship of Swiss-made mechanical watches powered by springs was valued above the more accurate and much more affordable quartz watches.

These days, wrists sport vastly more efficient, multi-functional gadgets that accomplish myriad tasks.

They let us know where we are, what we can do and indeed, even who we are. Telling time is just one of the lesser used features of these miraculous devices.

Qs & As from the Clutter-Buster's Blog

Dear Clutter-Buster:

Can you clarify *The Vehicle Disposal Act* for me?

My wife and I have had two separate automobiles for many years as we both needed them for essential jobs in different cities. I have recently retired and, as I understand it, I must dispose of mine as the exemption to *The One Vehicle per Household Law* no longer applies. My wife still works and uses hers for that purpose six days a week.

If I get rid of my moto as per the edict, I will not have access to a private vehicle for those six days. I find it tiring to walk any distance, so I genuinely need my car.

Is there a clause in the Act that will allow me to keep it?

I appreciate any assistance that you can provide.

With my paltry pension I can't afford a lawyer and I have little patience for dealing with government responders, an oxymoron if I ever heard of one. - *anxious in Arcadia*

Dear Anxious in Arcadia:

I am confused as to why you are only now, after retiring, seeking advice on your predicament. Nonetheless, I will try to help.

Because the municipality of Arcadia complies with *The Global Atmospheric Enhancement Act* by offering bicycles and other forms of transit free of charge for residents, you might have difficulty extending your vehicle exemption.

And while it may be arduous to get efficient information from government staff, I recommend that you call them about your problem.

A legal aid clinic servicing low-income residents in Arcadia could assist if your combined family income is below a specific threshold.

I suggest that you contact them to find out if you qualify for free legal advice.

Random Notes on *The Decline*
The Garbage Resolution

Hey bloggos, here's some more offbeat history. Today, eco-activist Rochelle Hassly takes a look at garbage.

The current *Alchemy Law* and the Magic Nine program are built on the environmental initiatives, the so-called green programs, of the latter part of the 20th century.

Long before *The Decline* and *The Final Catastrophe*, activists badgered governments and corporations to embrace the 3 Rs - Reduce, Reuse, Recycle - in order to lessen the disastrous impact of escalating garbage production.

In those days, instead of seeing M9 receptacles on street corners, you would walk, or more likely drive, past garbage bags and trash cans filled with all sorts of M9 materials. All destined for garbage dumps.

Unbelievable as it now sounds, each week on designated days, people dragged out their trash onto the curbs in front of their homes. Then municipal trucks would pick up the refuse and take it to immense waste disposal facilities and landfill sites on the outskirts of the city.

People born after *The Great Resolve*, when rubbish was effectively banned by *The Prohibition of Waste Law*, are shocked to learn about "garbage days" and the enormous amounts of trash produced in the old Consumerite society.

They are also flabbergasted to hear that when the concept of the 3 Rs was first introduced, it was considered a crackpot idea, destined to fail.

Actually, the whole notion of salvage and recovery so severely challenged the prevailing ethos of overconsumption and the wasteful habits of Consumerites that it was greatly ridiculed. And to be sure, initially the amount of resources collected for recycling - starting with just newspapers, metal cans and glass bottles - wasn't worth the cost of picking the stuff up, never mind the expense of transforming them into other materials.

However as disposal sites and garbage dumps filled to capacity, and in fact overflowed, country after country mandated waste reduction laws. Sadly, these edicts proved to be too few, and far too late.

One early solution to the waste disposal problem was to transport the garbage produced by wealthy industrialized nations to underdeveloped Third World countries.

At first, these poor nations eagerly accepted the trash in exchange for large sums of money that bolstered their economies and raised their standards of living.

Soon they found themselves overwhelmed by the massive amounts of waste produced by the developed countries and were forced to prohibit the importation and transfer of refuse from external sources.

With no other solution in sight, government advisers and analysts were in the final stages of implementing laws to turn parklands, conservation areas and world heritage sites into gigantic garbage dumps when billionaire shipbuilder and steelmaker, Dr. Jonathan Bondit came up with The Garbage Resolution.

This scheme used enormous, steel freight containers to stash trash. These garbage-filled repositories were stored on colossal cargo ships that were then piloted to the middle of the world's oceans and abandoned.

As we know only too well, nothing good ever comes from the crime of abandonment and The Garbage Resolution was no remedy at all. Rather, it resulted in furthering the degradation of the world's oceans and waterways.

Many of the containers storing waste were constructed with extremely poor quality steel and their seams were defectively welded. Over time the toxic contents of these containers began seeping into the depths.

As well, the increasing number of violent hurricanes that resulted from global warming caused thousands of the orphan ships to overturn and sink, hurling their foul cargo to the ocean floor. There, many of the receptacles burst open, spilling their poisonous contents into the world's already polluted seas.

These calamities led to a cataclysmic destruction of fish and marine life, the consequences of which we are still living with today.

We now recognize that The Garbage Resolution turned into one of the central crimes against humanity that brought about *The Final Catastrophe*.

And the destructiveness of this offence continues to haunt us as many of the ships are still floating in the middle of our oceans, perpetually deteriorating and leaking pollutants.

Amy Speaks
How to Live your Life with Space to Spare

Hey blog followers, I've heard you. You love the Clutter-Buster Qs & As and so do I. Today as a treat, I'm posting the first part of a speech that Amy Anderson, who the New World Times calls our #1 Clutter-Buster, gave to a sold out audience this past November.

Amy is the author of The Clutter-Buster's Manifesto and

Freedom from Clutter - Amy Anderson's Guide to Living your Life with Space to Spare.

Good evening and thank you for inviting me to talk about how to live your life with space to spare.

As the author of the Clutter-Buster's blog, I answer questions every day about people's problems with their possessions. And amazingly enough, even after *The Great Resolve* and the implementation of *The Naked Law*, I still get hundreds of enquiries daily from around the world.

I want to tell you that my blog is a labour of love. And I do mean labour as I struggle over each and every response that I give. I worry each word because I know not only how critical my replies are, but also how desperate people are for reliable information.

I try to answer as many questions as I can, but I can't respond to all of them, not while holding down a full-time job and raising a family.

That's why I developed *The Clutter-Buster's Manifesto* and my e-guidebook, *Freedom from Clutter*. And that's one reason why I'm giving this speech tonight. So that as many of you as possible can find solutions to your concerns and benefit from my experience.

Before getting to the manifesto and telling you how to live blissfully unencumbered with things, I want to give you a bit of background about me and my blog so that you know who I am.

First, let me make it clear upfront who I'm not.

You can be assured that I write not as some government flack trying to curry favour with my supervisors. I'm not in the business of promoting the rules and regulations of the various laws and acts that were developed and passed after

The Final Catastrophe.

Nor am I a secret mouthpiece for any corporate entity although I have been approached by several firms who, when they saw how many hits the blog gets and how many followers I have (now more than three million), courted me.

Their invitations obviously raised my hackles and made me even more determined not to perform a PR function, hidden or otherwise.

As well, I decided not to accept any promotions on my site or outright sponsorship deals. Money be damned. Walk the talk, I say.

Nor do I speak for any special interest faction except perhaps for the movement, if there is one, of plain old-fashioned common sense.

And heaven forbid, I don't want to be perceived as some sort of organizational guru or de-cluttering celebrity running from paparazzi.

So I'll give you the bare facts about who I am.

I am a typical, middle-aged, married woman with three teenagers still living at home and a dog. My family and I dwell in a two-storey house with a basement and a two-car garage in a suburb of a large city in the Co-Americas.

We bought the property before the law against garages came into effect, but have not yet disassembled it or rented it out as living accommodation. Rest assured, it's on our to-do list.

And we know that if we were to sell the house, that garage would immediately become part of our must-do list as it would be a huge disincentive to potential purchasers.

So you may well ask how I got involved with writing an online clutter-busting advice column.

Not only did I have personal hands-on experience with

eliminating stuff in my own house when *The Naked Law* came into effect, but I also received one of the first degrees as a Professional Downsizer from U-Get-It U.

To graduate I took courses in organizational theory and practice, law, counselling and coaching. It may interest you to know that my thesis was: *The Burden of Things: An Ethical and Moral History of our Attachment to Stuff.*

My internship included advising, supporting and training a wide variety of clients. These included ordinary folk who were just trying to get a grip on their consumption habits and the more challenging, obsessive-compulsive collectors and DSM certified hoarders.

Along the way I received further accreditation from the newly formed Association of Downsizing Consultants and I adhere to their official code of conduct and ethics.

As most of you surely know, de-cluttering is an ongoing, lifelong activity at home, in business, and in our leisure pursuits.

As an aside, let me tell you that if any of you or your children are considering a career, I can assure you that there is never a lack of work or opportunities for Pro-Dos.

As a Pro-Do, I help many people wade through the maze of government bureaucracy, interpret the laws, and fill out inventories and other legal forms.

In my practice, I continue to counsel a select number of private individuals and corporations. Obviously, I can't tell you who they are as my dealings with my clients are strictly confidential.

On a more personal note, my husband and I have elderly parents, aunts and uncles. Over time I have gotten intimately involved with helping them weed through their belongings and move into smaller dwellings and care homes.

I admit that it has not been an easy task. As unrepentant, out-of-control Consumerites, that generation of our elders was greatly affected by the laws and restrictions that were implemented at the time of *The Great Resolve.*

And although their token gods may have been Ralph Nader and other expositors of corporate malpractice, they were shoppers from birth. Instead of "mama," "dada," and "kitty," the first words from many of their lips were "I want," "buy me," and "charge it."

As they came of age, they continued to pursue their lust for all things material and new. Therefore I believe that we must treat that generation with a great deal of compassion as they grew up in a society far different from ours today.

The Seven Crimes of Consumerism

Esteemed colleagues, after Envy and Gluttony we get to Greed, the third deadly offence of consumerism that I want to highlight in my presentation to you tonight.

Dante wrote that Greed is too much love of money and power. Avarice, graspingness, acquisitiveness, whatever you call it, this is the crime of endlessly wanting more. Desiring ever more wealth, status and influence. Being insatiable.

During *The Decline*, this evil infiltrated governments and global corporations at the highest levels. And over time the unconstrained avarice of those in positions of authority completely ruined numerous public institutions and private organizations.

Regrettably, many of us in government today witnessed first-hand just how this pervasive corruption resulted in the total breakdown of economic systems and the wholesale collapse of markets everywhere.

We watched with utter horror as unalloyed greediness ultimately caused both the failure of governments and the downfall of corporations worldwide.

And we vowed with *The Great Resolve* to never let this catastrophe happen again.

Therefore you who work in governments today will be pleased to know that crucial administrative and management tactics are in place to rein in power and prevent Greed from overtaking civilization a second time.

These days both governments and corporations have compulsory codes of ethics and critical behaviour standards. Strict, government-mandated limits have been established to control executive salaries, benefits and perks. Stringent constraints and restrictions apply across the board, from clerks to CEOs in businesses large and small.

And because moderation and generosity are proven antidotes to Greed, these two essential attributes formed the foundation for the new society created after *The Final Catastrophe*.

I encourage everyone in this audience of Government Advisors from around the world, you who work so closely with leaders, I urge you to actively promote the quality of restraint tempered with benevolence.

And at the same time to be ever vigilant against this invidious crime of Greed.

Because we take this offence so seriously, the UEW has established a comprehensive protocol and a complete arsenal of weapons, such as absolute transparency and systematic audits, to combat Greed.

And for those found guilty, punishment is swift with immediate firing, public confessions and permanent posting of the transgression on personal and corporate Face pages.

Sheri Does the Inventory Her Way!

Oh Steve, I do find it awfully draining to think about my beloved belongings. Truth be told, that's one reason why I've put off filling out the Essential Goods Inventory form for so long.

And even though I'm now telling your followers the stories of objects that I still own, it's all disconcerting. Because of course, the thing is not in isolation, and this is what the bureaucrats will never understand.

The story is never simple. Describing one artefact leads inevitably to another, and that other may still exist, even if only in our minds.

Like the blue kitchen table. It goes with the chairs, does it not? Table and chairs, chairs and table.

But it does not go with any of the chairs that I've been recounting - the wicker ones, the chaise lounge, the throne, the head-in-a-trap chair.

It does, and doesn't, relate.

For thirty-five years the table formed part of the same household, one chunk of the goods and chattels of that home.

Except the table actually went with the press-backed maple chairs. The well-turned ones carved with beavers that I also painted peacock blue on the back deck of our house on Westminster.

How many mental breakdowns came about when *The Naked Law* was put into effect?

Think about that. People having to decide - like King Solomon - do I keep this and get rid of that? And what about this and this and this?

How to choose? How many changes of mind? How many regrets? How many arguments?

Such sadness, such anxiety, such dissension, and all because of things. Our lust and greed for possessions.

We were advised to recognize and to acknowledge that objects were not animate. Items could be disposed of, and needed to be, for the very survival of civilization.

The world was overflowing with stuff when it should have been over-flowering. Our planet was all filled up with junk and about to burst.

The earth's terrain was covered with things, and even more absurdly, things to store things - lockers, warehouses, garages, parking lots. All these spaces taking up land meant for living.

All this material strangling Mother Earth who did not want, did not need, could not handle another thing.

I know the drafters of *The Naked Law* were right: *Naked you came into this world, naked you must leave it*. And I truly believe it.

I understand and accept that my emotional attachment to my possessions was, and is, wrong. And I have tried to overcome my compulsion.

Yes, I have kept items against the law, but I have not added to my collections since *The Great Resolve*. And I no longer covet or acquire new old things. That must count for something.

Still, I feel the need to expiate my past sins by revealing something about my life among worldly goods. But be forewarned: although I will crow about my hapless treasures, I am no nightingale.

My songs are not all pleasant melodies. They are more like cheerless, frog-throated dirges filled with a litany of lost memories, discarded hopes, and unrealized dreams.

Museum of the Obsolete - Face Masks

Air pollution reached near epidemic intensities during *The Decline* forcing everyone all around the world to wear masks over their mouths and noses in order to breathe outdoors. The face protectors prevented toxic chemicals from entering people's lungs and destroying their health.

Sales of these assistive devices naturally skyrocketed in those gloomy years.

However, indicative of the unrestrained consumerism of that period, what should have been utilitarian safety gear developed into popular fashion accessories.

Luxurious designer and couturier masks were available in an outlandish variety of colours and assorted breathable fabrics. Both stylish and glitzy, they were much sought after and exorbitantly priced.

But face masks proved to be only a temporary panacea. Smog continued to blanket the planet reaching unbearable concentrations of contamination by the time of *The Final Catastrophe*.

By then too, the rates of lung cancer and pulmonary disease and the fatalities associated with them had advanced to disastrous levels.

Qs & As from the Clutter-Buster's Blog

Dear Clutter-Buster:

My folks are getting old and seem to be becoming more maudlin. At least my husband and I are noticing that they're making increasingly whiny demands. And we don't quite know how to handle it.

For instance, they keep trying to pass things on to us. Like when we were having dinner at their place, they would give us leftovers not in biodegradable containers, but in one of their fine china bowls or expensive, Swedish-made pots.

Then they would refuse to take back the receptacle when we had finished the food and tried to return it to them. They denied that it was their container and said that we must be mistaken.

We humoured them and kept the containers as we had some room in our allotment.

But now they want us to take more and more objects, treasures they call them, which they've kept un-inventoried and hidden away in drawers and cupboards. And they get all weepy when we refuse.

How can we turn down their gifts without hurting their feelings? - *fed up and frustrated*

Dear Fed Up and Frustrated:

Above all else, be kind.

The older generation was the most affected when *The Naked Law* was enacted. That age group had an extremely hard time disposing of the mass of products that they had accumulated over all their years of rampant, and I must say, government encouraged, conspicuous consumption.

They suffered greatly in trying to break lifetime habits, compulsions and addictions. And naturally, some were more successful at changing than others.

You may be surprised to learn that many elders, like your parents, did not fully follow the rules and regulations. In fact, some actually put barriers in the way.

A lot of people dragged out submitting their inventory forms way past the deadlines, and then declined to pay fines when challenged. Frequently they claimed that they could not understand the gobbledygook of the law, even though it was specifically written in clear and plain language.

Others contested at great length, the legalities of every single corollary to the Acts.

This resulted in an enormous number of appeals and amendments that in the long run created a much more complex legal system than the Controllers ever wanted.

So while I congratulate you on absorbing some of your parents' possessions into your allotment, you are right to be alarmed by the escalation of their requests.

To be sure, gifting used to be considered a positive and unselfish habit. We now know that to be totally wrong. But it seems as if your folks did not fully learn, or buy into, the new world view.

You must take the lead here. I suggest reversing roles and becoming your parents' parent. Stress that while you know they are trying to be kind, their generosity could get you into a lot of trouble.

And try to get them to think of innovative ways to get rid of their stuff before they pass on. You definitely do not want to be saddled with disposing of their possessions, especially the illegal ones, after their demise.

A Chorus of Voices - Obsolescence No More!

A lot of people gripe about *The Great Resolve's* 1,666, but you have to acknowledge that some truly important laws are buried in there. Edicts that'll save us from ever having to go through a catastrophe again.

One of my out-and-out favourites is *The Abolition of Built-In Obsolescence Act*. How could anybody not like this?

Still, when it was enacted, stock prices fell and the global economy threatened to collapse once more.

Unquestionably, change happens when innovations like automobiles or computers replace buggies and typewriters, for example. What was despicable and led to the Act was not this kind of progress, but rather planned obsolescence.

Greedy companies had for decades deliberately designed products to stop functioning after a pre-determined period of time in order to accelerate sales. And when stuff inevitably broke down, it often cost more to repair the items than to buy new ones.

You can well imagine how all those damaged goods increased the amount of garbage. And how manufacturing replacement parts wasted our limited natural resources.

Fashion was the other big reason that people threw out perfectly serviceable items and I'm not just talking about clothes here. Appliances were often trashed just because some hotshot designer gurus suggested that there was a more "in" colour.

In fact, conglomerates of trade associations regularly conspired to predict and promote the next trend in colour and style. Aqua blue and minimalist lines this year. Chocolate brown and bulky contours next season.

Stupidly, people who wanted modern homes and swanky decor spent their hard earned money trying to keep up, like gerbils on a wheel.

Laszlo the Fixer

As I understand it, governments during The Decline made it difficult for you Fixers to do your jobs. Can you tell us a bit about that? What kind of pressure did they put on you?

During that time, governments were aggressively promoting outsourcing and trade exchanges with Third World countries whose use of cheap labour made it next to impossible for local workers to compete.

Part of the administrations' not-so-hidden agenda was to farm out production abroad while also purchasing enormous quantities of shoddy, foreign-made merchandise.

And at the same time, more and more environmentally conscious consumers were buying less, and having their old or broken items refurbished.

This seemed to interfere with the authorities' plans, so they added outrageous taxes to repair services.

With these extra taxes, fixing anything became way more costly than buying brand new. And I suspect that's what Big Biz wanted all along.

Not only that, but suddenly all Fixers had to be registered and required expensive licences to operate. Now we needed accreditation and certificates attesting to our expertise.

We had to pass annual tests of our technical skills and were subject to relentless scrutiny by government watchdogs and abusive auditors.

Still more detrimental than these additional charges and rules was the seemingly unlimited power of corporations to influence consumers to crave and buy the latest, trendy trinkets and state-of-the-art goods.

And in point of fact, countless marketing budgets rivalled the gross national production of entire small countries.

Advertising was constantly in your face.

Absolutely no place, not even churches, hospitals or nursery schools, was free of consumer messages blasting away 24/7.

And you couldn't turn on any device without being

bombarded with noisy intrusive hype.

Everything new was associated with the good life, with success, and with happiness. Why would anyone in their right mind pay to fix something when they could get a pristine thing for so much less?

Old stuff was bad news. It was gauche, in poor taste. Antiques were junk. Shabby was no longer chic. Revamped goods were ridiculed. You would have to be insane to value an outmoded item so much as to repair it.

So the throwaway society became the norm.

Sheri Does the Inventory Her Way!

Enough about chairs. Now I'll tell you about another discovery of mine from the 19th century. I came across this one at an antique store in the village of Lakefield near the family cottage, when second homes were still allowed.

We were up for a weekend and went into town to buy fresh homemade bread and butter tarts. Being collectors, we couldn't resist popping into the local antique shop.

Like many visitors to such places, we weren't looking for anything specific. We were just browsing, passing the time and delighting in finding odds and ends from earlier eras.

Almost completing a circuit of the store, having peered into all its nooks and crannies, gotten down on my knees (those were the days) to scrutinize an old etching propped on the floor, rummaged through many a box of ephemera, I suddenly glimpsed just a shard of a green ceramic tile.

Lifting away a planter, I was surprised to unearth a fully tiled splash-back on a marble-topped washstand. Removing still more stuff heaped haphazardly on it revealed, most wonderfully, that the tiles were in perfect condition and featured two exquisite, stylized water lilies.

I knew instantly that we had to have this splendid piece.

Those were the days when dealers would buy, sight unseen, containers of antiques from Britain and Europe. This washstand had been part of such a cache and so, sadly, there was no personal history attached to it.

Its provenance though was thought to be England. Its design and the tiles suggested that it belonged to the Art Nouveau period of 1890-1910. And without a doubt, its elegant simplicity and curved lines wholly reflected the essence of that artistic movement.

Such was the intensity of my desire that I never really considered the difficulties that purchasing such an antiquated piece of furniture would entail.

I was assailed by a feeling of acquisitiveness so severe that I never stopped, stepped back and said rationally, "Hey wait a minute, let's sleep on this and come back tomorrow."

No such sensible phrase passed my fevered lips. Nor did I pause in my excited enthusiasm to consider the price, or the fact that our tiny car did not have a trunk big enough to cart the prize home. And where in our tiny bedsitter was I going to put this outmoded item?

Nonetheless, I had to scratch this absurd itch. So I did. We bought the striking piece and spent the drive back to the cottage rationalizing our newest acquisition and figuring out how we would get it home.

In retrospect, I am amazed at our spontaneous action. Was it because we had spent an hour looking at charming knick-knacks and bric-a-brac without seeing anything at all that was appealing enough to buy?

We had, in fact, finished our tour of the store and would have left empty-handed were it not for this find.

Or was it because we were so carefree (um, perhaps careless) in a future-be-damned way that only those young and in love can be?

Whatever. The deed was done.

It went unpunished and was never subject to typical love spats of regret and recrimination. Instead it became our most cherished possession, moving with us from house to house to where it now graces the arts and crafts hallway of what is probably our final abode.

Never sullied with expensive ornaments, we let the washstand's beauty shine through, even as it served as a practical catch-all for those markers of daily life - keys and coins, hats and gloves, bags and boxes. A veritable pedestal of the mundane once again!

The Seven Crimes of Consumerism

Now we come to the fourth of the deadly offences - the crime of Lust. And here, in the context of consumerism, we mean not impetuous sexual desire, but rather Lust for things.

Yes, I'm talking about impulsive acquisitiveness and reckless materialism. About voraciously desiring ever more possessions and about hankering after all sorts of objects that we don't really need. Wanting to satisfy our every craving, hunger and yearning for stuff.

Indeed, such insatiable Lust can be seen in all the other crimes that I'm enumerating in my address here today.

Lust is the driving force behind so many misdeeds and so much misery. That's why such unlawful longing must be severely curtailed and controlled if we are to maintain the moderate society that we now enjoy.

Numerous books and treatises have been written on how

to tame the crime of unbridled Lust, so I'll mention just a few proven deterrents here.

One excellent method - compulsory cooling-off periods - has been shown to effectively curb this irresponsible crime.

Another particularly successful constraint on excessive desire is filling out the Needs Analysis for Any Purchase in Excess of Allotment form for review by the Department against Overconsumption.

Finally, *The Law in Praise of the Non-Unique* and the associated Awards for the Ordinary, Everyday and Familiar provide positive reinforcement against this devious crime.

Museum of the Obsolete
Trade Fair Giveaways

The trading and selling of merchandise has played an integral role in civilization's progress, and also in its decline. This can be seen through the evolution of trade fairs from purely practical enterprises to elaborate dog and pony shows.

In the middle ages, makers of all sorts of goods regularly gathered at fairs in towns to display and market their wares.

And periodically in the 19th and 20th centuries, world expositions were held in major cities to showcase the latest industrial and technological innovations.

By the 21st century however, trade shows had evolved into immense, specialized commercial marketplaces where hucksters hawked an unlimited number of manufactured products, most of which were indistinguishable from each other, and totally unnecessary.

At these events, promotional giveaways that shamelessly drew attention to a company's or an organization's logo and brand were everywhere.

These frivolous freebies included a colossal amount of such extraneous items as t-shirts, stress balls, coasters, hats, badges, buttons, mugs, glasses, bottles, openers, pens, bags, notebooks, and calendars.

Most of these gizmos were ephemeral, quickly broke or ended up stashed away, with dozens of others, in drawers and in closets before eventually being thrown out.

Astonishingly too, some greedy consumers also collected this so-called "advertising memorabilia," resulting in the emergence of an entire secondary market for trading and selling this useless junk.

Needless to say, all marketing giveaways were forbidden under *The Banning of Gratuitous Advertising Law*.

And nowadays at approved events, people wear their own clothes and bring their own sani-cups for tap water, and tabs or recorders for note-taking.

Ultimately, *The Essential Goods Only Act* put an end to all trade fairs.

Today's conferences are strictly controlled. Organizers must justify the need for these events on their Statements of Essentiality for Congresses and get prior approval from the Department against Overconsumption.

Qs & As from the Clutter-Buster's Blog

Dear Clutter-Buster:

When I was putting my 14-year-old son's underwear and socks in his dresser drawer, I found a small box filled with a jumble of rubbish - cracked buttons, shards of glass, bottle caps, paper wrappings and broken pieces that seemed to be from various tech devices.

It was tucked way back under a pile of t-shirts. I fear that this may signal a hoarding compulsion. Do you think this is just a phase that he will outgrow?

I don't want to risk alienating him as we have a good rapport. - *worried mom*

Dear Worried Mom:

I don't think that questioning your son will enhance your relationship at all. In fact, doing so is more likely to cause irreparable damage as he will probably be uncomfortable with the idea of you rummaging through his belongings.

Adolescents need a sense of privacy, and ownership of their own things to develop into secure trusting adults. So while I realize that having a box is illegal, I recommend not saying anything about your discovery.

The concern that I have though is not with your son, but rather with you. I suggest that you examine your own actions closely. Ask yourself what caused you to pry. I can see doing so if you suspected illicit drug use, for example, but your missive indicated no such worry.

The fault, dear worried mom, lies within you. *Gnothe se* - know thyself.

A Chorus of Voices
Mick Volunteers at the Care Palace

I was doing my unpaid work stint. You know I drew the wild card, but it ain't so bad. Hey, I got to talk to the old geezers. At least, the ones who still remember how to speak and the ones who can talk in English.

Yeah, no kidding, some people when they get really old

- I'm saying like mid-nineties here - they forget how to talk. Others speak in foreign tongues.

One women was born here, raised here, lived all her life here, talking English like a normal person, and then wham, she's suddenly nattering away in Hungarian.

Turns out when she was little she heard her grandparents speak to her father in Hungarian and somewhere in her brain that language was like stored, and ninety years later it came out. Wow, no shit, yeah man, frickin' weird, I'd say.

Then there was this old fart who said he was a bounty-hunter. No, not from the old west. He meant a bargain-hunter, but not for real either, although they called it Reality TV way back in the days before.

He was an actor on a TV show called *Storage Mania,* and the synop was that bidders had ten minutes to scope out the contents of a repossessed and forgotten storage unit before the auction started. The winning bidder could walk away with a heap of trash, or a treasure trove.

So anyway, every time I got to push him around in his wheelchair, he would go on and on about the things that he had found in these lockers. He said that the contents were genuine, nothing planted for the sake of the show.

And he told how a lot of the programs were super boring 'cause most of the compartments did have only junk in them. Crap he said, like run-down exercise equipment, old clothes, mouldy books and broken bikes.

One time though, he bid on a bolted unit where he could only see some rusty old filing cabinets - the kind that they used to have for keeping paper files. Way cool, eh?

Anyhow, bounty-hunter bid and he got it for fifty bucks. He figured that the metal alone melted down would be worth a lot more than that.

When he went to empty the cabinets, he discovered that some of the files had unopened Christmas and birthday cards filled with cash. No BS, he cleared a grand that day. Is that smart, or what?

Another time, he bid twenty dollars on a locker full of boxes - books and magazines mostly - but hidden in the back under them all was a scooter worth hundreds!

The dude said that for what people had paid in storage fees, they could have bought new stuff many times over.

And he now thought that if you had to rent a storage locker for more than a couple of months, you had way too much stuff. He could see that people should have let their possessions go in favour of what was truly important, like friends and adventures.

The guy said that he thought *The Naked Law* made a lot of sense. He showed me how he was now down to one room with just his clothes in a small chest of drawers and a three-shelf cupboard hung in the corridor beside his doorway. And he told me that he felt just fine with that.

He never looked at the three-shelver when I was there and on my visits I didn't pay attention to it either. But once after I had taken him back to his room for a nap, I clicked on my cell and snapped a pix of it.

Not long after, I went to visit the dude, but they told me that he had passed and assigned me to another inmate. This time, a granny who didn't talk much at all.

It was that night that I looked at the picture I had taken of the bounty-hunter's cabinet and wished that I had asked him about the stuff in it. The few trinkets that I saw were an odd mix - a couple of rings, a glass paperweight, a fishing-fly, some rusty keys, an old watch and a carved wooden bird.

A half dozen small framed photos filled the rest of the

shelves and some loose ones were tacked to the back and sides of the cupboard. Oddly enough, none of the pix were of things; they were all of people or animals. And for all his bounty-hunting talk, not one showed him as a TV star.

I wondered who the people in the pictures were, and why he had valued those particular bits and pieces enough to keep them. I know that size determined a lot - he couldn't put a scooter on a shelf, even if that was one of his biggest finds. But still, I wished that I'd asked. Now it was too late.

When I next visited Granny M, I videoed her cubby-hole and asked her about the items in it. And no crap, once she started talking about her *wee* things she couldn't stop. I soon knew more about her life than her grand-kids probably did.

From there, I just started the project, shooting all the other three-shelvers that lined the walls in the old people's palace and interviewing their curators.

Sure, I was sorta interested, but it also didn't hurt that I needed an essay for social history. So I submitted my video - *Memory Boxes: Cabinets of Curious Artefacts of the Past*. It only took me a few days, and I got a frickin' A.

All in all, my volunteering paid off for me. Nah, really, I kinda liked the bounty-hunter and was sad when he passed. Granny M, too - she was a neat old lady.

Random Notes on *The Decline* - Air Pollution

Hey blogsters, today Tobias Green provides some interesting info about air pollution.

As early as 2013, scientists verified what many commuters choking on smog had long suspected - air pollution was a carcinogen.

The toxic particles in the atmosphere burrowed deep into people's lungs causing cancer and pulmonary disease.

At that time, the International Agency for Research on Cancer said that it considered airborne contaminants to be the most significant environmental cancer-causing agent.

It further reported that the main sources of pollution were pervasive. They included transportation, power plants, and industrial and agricultural emissions.

Dramatic differences in air quality were noted among cities around the world. The most noxious metropolises were in India and China, where people frequently wore face masks outdoors to protect themselves.

Ironically, only when the report was issued and experts found that the country's thick smog damaged tourism did China frantically introduce new efforts to curb pollution.

As their economies suffered, other nations also adopted stricter controls on spewing fumes in a last-ditch attempt to curb the pending calamity.

However, the largest manufacturing countries globally continued to produce record-breaking amounts of toxic pollution throughout *The Decline*.

In fact, the mass destruction of humanity's most essential resource, the air we breathe, ultimately closed down major cities, crippled the international economy, and led directly to *The Final Catastrophe*.

During *The Great Resolve*, the United Entities of the World enacted stringent restrictions and regulations on the atmosphere to safeguard against such an environmental disaster ever happening again.

At that time the global government body also began the lengthy and arduous process of revitalizing the earth's land masses and waterways, humankind's other vital assets.

78

Sheri Does the Inventory Her Way!

As I write another entry in preparation for my defence Steve, my eyes alighted on two rocks on my desk that I wasn't able to list on the official inventory form because there was no category for them.

Oh yes, I could have listed them under Miscellaneous, but that would be such a misnomer. They were not some sundry items that belonged in a category like Assorted or Other. They were not afterthoughts. Far from it.

These unique pieces were selected with much care and carried from a foreign locale at an equally exotic time of my life to rest in a place of honour on my desk in the series of homes that I have lived in.

Yet were you to take a cursory glance at these rough-hewn stones, you might well shrug and wonder what I saw in them and question why I carted them with me from place to place over the years.

I suppose though, like most special objects, their value comes from the many associations and memories embedded in my mind and released whenever I hold these two precious rocks in my hands and let the sunlight caress them.

My husband and I were students bound on a voyage of discovery in North Africa while travelling abroad for a year. We had packed lightly and agreed to buy few souvenirs and only those that we could easily carry.

The bus taking us along the ancient trade route from Fez to Marrakech had stopped at a roadside café where a turban-headed Berber crouched alongside a mountain of rocks. A hand-scrawled sign indicated one dirham, a price that we could afford.

I spent a long time looking over this precious pile and

only the imminent departure of the bus made me swiftly choose the two small, glittery fragments that I take such pleasure in today.

The larger nugget was streaked with deposits of white, ecru and coral-coloured minerals topped by diamond-like crystals sprinkled with bits of mica. The smaller, L-shaped gem contained a large band of amethyst permeated with serpentine veins of opal and iron.

These two simple rocks are reminders of the first trip that we ever made together as a couple.

And for me, they also represent our youthful days of exploration and adventure when we were fresh with curiosity and boundless enthusiasm. When everything we saw was not as if for the first time, but was, in reality, unprecedented. When every object had in it the possibility of astonishment.

I perceive these misshapen crystalline pieces as jewels ripped from the underworld, my own personal Persephones. And I can picture Hobbit-like miners working deep under the Atlas mountains of Morocco laboriously carrying the stones in sacks on their backs to the surface. Then heaping them on the ground and releasing them from the dark into the light.

And every time I look at them, it amazes me to think that these two shards were once part of the bedrock of the earth, hidden underground and invisible to us as we obliviously went about our daily business above.

And I realize too, how often in life we are only aware of externals and miss the gemstones unless we dig deep.

These two rocks, although miniscule in relationship to the earth's crust from which they were cut, remain awe-inspiring artefacts in themselves, and I think they are quite magical.

They are able - *abracadabra* - to transform me not only to a time long ago when we were young and carefree, but also to the eternal present. For their solidity and their unchangeable nature remind me to value the durability and stability of my long-lasting marriage as well.

Museum of the Obsolete - Eyeglasses

Before *The Final Catastrophe*, most people with vision problems wore curved pieces of glass over their eyes. The glass was custom-made to correct particular sight defects and held in place with lightweight metal or plastic frames that wrapped around a person's ears.

The frames had evolved from practical wire mechanisms into trendy accessories available in an ever-changing range of materials, styles and colours. And because of the fashion component, eyeglasses, which should have been simple and inexpensive medical devices, expanded into a $30 billion global market during *The Decline*.

The Great Resolve eliminated superfluous manufactured products and mandated free laser surgery to correct vision deficiencies. This completely did away with eyeglasses, except for sunglasses and safety glasses which were allowed under Exemption 0133645kj for Manufactured Products Required for Safety Purposes.

Qs & As from the Clutter-Buster's Blog

Dear Clutter-Buster:

My boyfriend for the past 18 months and I have been discussing sharing an apartment, but we keep getting into terrible arguments while trying to complete the form for Amalgamating Two Households into One.

He feels that every one of his things should be kept while mine could easily be disposed of. He says that my stuff isn't as good as his.

I find this upsetting because it's just not true. Do you think we have a future as a couple? - *just wondering*

Dear Just Wondering:

You are lucky that filling out this form has exposed his domineering nature early in your relationship.

Before you make the big commitment of living together in one dwelling, I strongly recommend that you take a step back. You need to probe deeper, perhaps with a counsellor, to learn if your boyfriend has more underlying control and possession issues.

Laszlo the Fixer

So the Fixers' values clashed with those of consumers?

Yeah, big time. You have to realize that the era was rife with overconsumption. Everything was about buying power. Buy more, buy up, buy often. By spending you were helping the economy, you were creating jobs, you were a good citizen. Blah, blah, blah.

And the majority of people bought into this claptrap whole-hog. Except some of us, crafters and artists mostly, hated this barefaced commercialism.

We were appalled by throwing away perfectly good, still working items just because new-fangled things had been produced in the latest colours or with minimal refinements to their design and were heavily promoted.

We abhorred planned obsolescence - the whole concept

of building malfunctions into products, so that their useful life was shortened. As soon as warranties were up, things fell apart. It was exasperating and totally stupid.

In many cases, cell phones are a good example, the price of a battery or replacement part exceeded the cost of getting a brand new item with up-to-the-minute features. But if you got the latest model, none of the old accessories and software would work with it, so then you had to buy different add-ons as well. Sheer corporate greed.

Well Steve, we rebelled. We decided to live a simple life, to subsist within our means, to do with less. We got rid of our TVs and we sold our cars. We took to walking and biking instead. This was way before *The Great Resolve* and the mandated extinction of most private vehicles.

We downsized long in advance of it becoming law. We revived home cooking and sewing one's own clothes - even though, or perhaps because, cheap clothing was being manufactured by poorly paid workers, slaves, I'd say, in criminally unsafe conditions in Third World countries.

Our revolt was based on not wanting to spend one's time doing mundane work just to survive.

A sort of hippie culture returned. Back to the land, grow your own food, communal gardening - that kind of thing. And naturally, in that environment, making things by hand and repairing stuff were necessary.

As well, entire communities sprung up in isolated pockets all over the world as a backlash to capitalism. The Gabriola and Hornby islands in British Columbia and the cities of Portland, Oregon and Key West, Florida were home to some of the first Fixer enclaves in North America.

And because of the web, we could share these new-old philosophies and provide tips on opting out. Buy nothing days, weeks and months were common online challenges.

I loved that whole way of being and so, like many others, I became a committed Fixer. And, in fact, I never took a factory job again.

That obviously riled the hard-working 9-to-5ers, the Consumerites. They accused us of wanting a welfare state, of being commies, of living off their wages, of not doing a good day's work, but expecting government hand-outs. More blather.

The Seven Crimes of Consumerism

Envy, Gluttony, Greed, and Lust lead us to Pride, the fifth crime of consumerism.

You all know the ancient aphorism "pride goeth before a fall." Well, arrogance definitely had pride of place in society before *The Final Catastrophe* and we must ensure that it does not get elevated to an admired trait ever again.

One of the major transgressions of consumerism, Pride must not be tolerated. Conceit, smugness, superiority, self-importance, whatever you call it, this grievous offence is the opposite of humility.

This odious crime would be totally incomprehensible to the many esteemed individuals who have made outstanding contributions to civilization. People like Mahatma Gandhi, Mother Teresa, Nelson Mandela, Saint Frank, and Laszlo Lorca, to name just a few.

Everyone, and I include everybody in this audience here tonight, must ask themselves what they are most proud of.

You don't have to share this insight with anyone, but once you've identified what you feel superior about, I ask you to examine it from every angle. Analyse why you feel smug and how that self-importance manifests itself.

Then I urge you to discard it. Throw it away. Purge yourself of shameful Pride.

Be humble. Consider that whatever was filling your mind with vanity was closing your heart to countless others - from your mother and father to your teachers and co-workers - everyone who helped you get to where you are today. Who helped you achieve whatever you are so proud of.

Remember that you did not accomplish anything in isolation. In the words of the great poet John Donne: "No man is an island."

Because you are only one person in an intricate web of community, there is no room for arrogance either in your life or in our society. And certainly not in the governments that you serve.

That's why the United Entities of the World, recently introduced *The Count Your Blessings Regulation* and *The Thank You Act*. And I can tell you that the implementation of these laws in the workplace and by families in their homes has already significantly lessened the offence of Pride.

I invite you to take a close look at these laws and bring them back to your local authorities. If they do not yet have similar initiatives in place, then I ask you to encourage your governments to immediately adopt them.

Amy Speaks
How to Live your Life with Space to Spare

Many of you have asked me how my labour of love, the Clutter-Buster's blog, came about. I will admit that I took a somewhat circuitous route to get there.

Through a combination of my professional downsizing practice and my work with friends and relatives, I saw the need for concrete guidelines to help people rid themselves of their possessions. Once I developed a short list of rules for my clients, I posted it on my website and asked for feedback.

The response to that call for comments was amazing, and frankly, quite overwhelming. I got suggestions galore along with a plethora of unsolicited specific queries. Important, personal and anxious questions.

I wanted to help, but didn't know where to begin. So many problems, so much confusion, so little time.

As an interim measure - a sort of crisis response team of one - I launched the Clutter-Buster's blog.

On the blog I could answer people's most pressing questions in-depth and give sound advice derived from my specialized training and my hands-on experience.

And by posting the questions and my answers online, everyone with similar problems would benefit.

At the same time I started to create a manifesto based on my own philosophy of de-cluttering that would outline some comprehensive theories for divesting one's self and one's environment of things.

My goal was to limit these tenets to ten.

As I was responding to questions on my blog and fleshing out my manifesto, I decided that a practical how-to, step-by-step instruction guide for de-cluttering would prove useful. Such a manual would assist people with their day-to-day activities, give them freedom from clutter, and allow them to enjoy a life unencumbered by stuff.

It was, and is, my fervent hope that after reading my e-guidebook, people would be able to live full lives with plenty of space to spare.

I can't tell you why, but I felt a powerful urge to make it simpler for folk to stick to the precepts of *The Naked Law*. And I sensed that I could best accomplish that mission through my blog, my manifesto and my e-guidebook.

Soon enough, I recognized that I had truly found my life purpose. It was as if everything I'd ever done up to that time was leading me to these three communication tools.

However, I will admit here, for the record, that realizing this calling did not come without costs.

As you know if you've ever set up a blog, especially an interactive one, you're embarking on a time-sucker of huge proportions.

Some questions submitted read like rants. Others were condescending. A few contained litigious racist or sexist statements. So I was forced to make tough decisions about each and every query.

As well, nearly all of the submissions that I received needed to be rigorously edited for clarity before posting.

It's as if people were so anxious about getting replies that they couldn't be bothered checking the grammar and spelling of their questions.

And writing briefly is darn hard work as every tweeter knows. Concise, easy-to-read questions and answers only get that way through great effort.

Consequently, every single Q & A on my blog had to be carefully crafted through many drafts and rewrites.

And although I didn't appreciate it at the start, coming up with succinct and pithy responses turned out to be an enormous undertaking.

Moreover by going public with a blog, I was putting my reputation online with every answer I gave.

A blog post by its very nature seems ephemeral, one

dispatch quickly replaced by the next, so you could suppose that the writing doesn't much matter.

However as you know, every post is permanent. And as a pro, I wanted to ensure that all my responses would stand the test of time, and the scrutiny of future readers.

As a result, working on my blog soon swallowed up any semblance of a social or home life.

My husband, who has an intense career of his own, could truly understand and put up with the requirements of my burgeoning new endeavour. It also helped that he has a take it or leave it attitude towards social engagements.

I gave them up, albeit more reluctantly, as I became obsessed with my work.

Our teens continued to be oblivious to us in general - surfacing from their devices only when necessary to eat, groom and go to school.

Once the blog went viral though, they thought it was pretty cool having a virtual celeb mom.

Because of time constraints, I had to turn down new clients. This hit me financially although I still resolved to keep my blog free of corporate promos and sponsorships.

And today, with speaking engagements, lectureships and skyrocketing sales of my e-guidebook, I've more than made up for any economic hardships that I encountered in sticking to my principles.

So I think you can see how the Clutter-Buster's blog is at the heart of everything I do, say and write.

I know too, that it is a lifeline to my three million fans - some of who are in the audience here tonight.

And I understand that it is also proving its worth to the many people - more than fifty every hour - who are only now discovering it.

Sheri Does the Inventory Her Way!

To the east of Morocco lay the origins of my next treasure, a stunning example of glass art from the city of Mdina on the island of Malta.

I admire this particular piece of glass above all the other vases and paperweights that I have collected, and I don't think that you could find a finer sample of this ancient craft anywhere. No, not even in Venice.

It has pride of place in the window cove of my kitchen, so that I can see its Mediterranean blue glow, most especially when I am washing dishes. But my eyes savour it whenever I am in that cozy room which, not surprisingly, is the go-to gathering place in our home.

And over the years, my kitchen has been filled with much more than idle chitchat and amusing banter.

It's where the most important conversations of my life have happened. Discussions that weren't just about cooking or eating, but about living - sometimes affirming, other times depressing, and frequently life changing.

Should Jonathan quit his job, give up the security of a regular pay cheque and health insurance and strike out on his own? What should we do about Jeremy and his decision to join the army? Who's going to take care of dad now that mom has died?

Somehow answers to questions such as these became obvious the more one cleaned and peeled, chopped and stirred, wiped and tossed. The whirr of the food processor or garbage disposal and the hum of the refrigerator in some way led to clearer thoughts.

A sip of wine and a nibble of cheese helped, too.

Yes, it would be OK for Karen to fly 3,000 miles to the

other end of the country to visit her boyfriend and his parents at that most perfect of family times, Christmas.

And when conversations got heated, debates raged into anger and talk turned cold, it was a blessed relief to glance up at the window and see that free-form sculpture of glass sitting serenely in its alcove.

A piece of exquisite glass has a magical and spiritual effect on me. I am first of all fascinated by the alchemy of glass-making - how common grains of sand are transformed into a liquid and then into a solid mass of beauty through the skills of a talented artisan.

And the technique of blowing through a pipe and inflating molten glass into a fragile bubble moves the entire process into yet another dimension.

It is truly wondrous how these magicians use their breath, that vital life force that's common to all of us, to fashion a delicate form that literally takes one's breath away.

The entire procedure reverberates with primal mysticism. And even though I'm not a Christian, I can't help but relate glass-making to the depiction of God in *Genesis* creating man with a mouthful of air.

I also think of philosopher Mircea Eliade who, in a book that my sister gave me, described how objects, through the sacred act of their mysterious creation, manifest themselves in an otherworldly way in our profane world.

And in the inspired design of my Mdina glass, I see a fineness that goes far beyond its perfect technique to fully embrace the intuitive vision of its creator. For its abstract shape was formed not from a pattern or a mould, but purely by the lungful of air and the beating heart of the artisan who conceived it.

So for me this divine object, that I take such pleasure in,

is full of soul, containing the essence of its maker.

Such is, I believe, the power of things in general. And why it is so difficult to try to relegate them to just a title on an inventory form. A piece of blue glass - what indeed does that tell you?

It also boggles my mind that the earliest evidence of the revolutionary concept of blowing glass came from fragments of glass tubes dumped in a ritual bath in Jerusalem sometime around 4 BC.

Yes, archaeologists rummaging around a dump stumbled upon the origins of this ancient craft. That's just one more example of what relics reveal about our ancestors.

And I suppose that such archaeological discoveries also serve as a worthwhile precedent to my relentless salvaging of objects. Vindication if I ever needed it.

The Great Resolve prohibited amassing collections and I think that this was a crucial decision in light of the outrageous wrong-doings inherent in the doomed society before *The Final Catastrophe*.

Yet I can't help but feel that this banning led to a great loss, too. Artefacts have taught us so much.

I hope that in the future our culture will have recovered enough, so that government mandated restrictions can be re-examined, and perhaps loosened.

Museum of the Obsolete
Cash Forms of Money

Coinage (shrapnel) and paper notes (bills) were physical tokens used as currency - commonly referred to as money or cash - for centuries before *The Final Catastrophe*.

Their function goes back to ancient times when metals representing the value of commodities formed the basis of trade. Pieces of copper, silver and gold were the most common coinage. With the introduction of printing, pieces of paper representing value became widespread.

And in many monetary systems, copper coins were the smallest denomination. Most countries stopped production of these "pennies" during *The Decline* when it turned out to be more expensive to make them than they were worth.

The elimination of other coins and paper notes soon followed as cash transactions declined and virtual money commerce became customary.

Qs & As from the Clutter-Buster's Blog

Dear Clutter-Buster:

My husband is intense, brilliant and loving and a good father to our son. He can also be hot-tempered which is why I'm asking for your advice.

I recently found in an unsealed closet in his private office a stash of acoustic guitars - the kind no longer made or even played in our electro age. I know he doesn't have permission for this collection since we have already used up our dispensations for my vintage dolls and his model cars.

Should I ask him about this or just forget it? I worry about the effect of his offence on our son if he were to find them. - *not wanting trouble*

Dear Not Wanting Trouble:

You don't say if your husband's volatility could lead to physical abuse or violence. Nor do you explain how you came about your discovery. Were you snooping?

If that was the case, it may increase his anger. I would consider these two issues before questioning him about his accumulation of guitars.

If you do decide to probe, you may want to suggest your concern for your son as the reason for your curiosity.

Tell him also that as his wife, you are legally responsible for his possessions and his transgressions if he were to die before you.

A Chorus of Voices
The Sad Tale of Wee Willy Magee

When *The Naked Law* came into effect they said we had to dispose of things that served no practical purpose. Anyhow, that covered a lot of the territory of my life - antiques and art. There was nothing useful about either of them.

Truthfully, I may as well have ended it then and there. And sadly, many people did, including poor old Willy.

Willy was one of those guys you used to see late at night before garbage day (if you remember that archaic, now extinct event) trolling the streets in his vehicle - in his case, a tricycle with a basket in back and a wagon lashed onto that.

Willy was after small finds, not the big pieces of furniture that people discarded. Those he left to the pickers in trucks and vans. He found it better to seek out his spoils by cycling, stopping, and then rummaging through the trash.

Some say that Willy was an artist - turning much of his loot into pieces of sculpture. I don't know about that.

I do remember though that he set up a table covered with his pickings outside his seniors' building and could be found there most mornings along with the smokers - a dying lot themselves. At least the banning of tobacco cut down on smoking deaths and vaping produced no dirty butts.

Anyhow, all this came to an abrupt end, ironically on the feast day of Saint Salvatore, the patron saint of salvagers. That was the day they enacted *An Act to Abolish Residential Garbage Collection* and *The Dumpster Prohibition Law*.

Wow, two legislative whammies pushed into law at the same time. Little did we know then that this was only the beginning. Over the course of six months, they would pass a total of 1,666 laws and acts, sometimes as many as a dozen in one day.

At first on nights after door-to-door trash pick-up ended, Willy, like an addict, would follow his usual route, slowing down in front of previous haunts, but stopping nowhere. It was as if a compulsion drove him to keep cycling up and down the same old blocks. It must have been tough for him.

But once block by block surveillance started, he stopped completely. I would sometimes see him on the benches in the safe havens just sitting - not hooked up to any electros - doing nothing, simply staring. It was creepy.

Then, no more Willy. Sad really!

Oddly enough on the streets where he used to regularly pass, people missed the sound of his squeaky old trike. The shrill clang that told them he was carting away their cast-offs and freeing them from the remorse of throwing stuff out.

The Seven Crimes of Consumerism

Now ladies and gentlemen, we come to Sloth, the sixth of the seven crimes of consumerism.

This offence basks in laziness, idleness and wasted time. Sloth is, without a doubt, at the core of a dissolute life.

Truly, there is no dignity in Sloth - only a pathetic, groaning sluggishness.

And as you may have observed, indolence and apathy are the hallmarks of this mostly hidden transgression.

Legally, this misconduct is hard to prosecute because of its covert nature. Nonetheless, it becomes all too visible when it leads to the misdemeanours of procrastination, wilful neglect, inactivity and obesity.

Sloth and the criminality emanating from it were all too evident during *The Decline*.

And the misdeeds were abetted by the convenience inherent in most product innovations of that era.

At that time, the quality of effortlessness was built into almost all merchandise. Ease of operation was relentlessly promoted as their primary, must-have selling feature.

A case could surely be made that all inventions and improvements in the 20th and early part of the 21st century were aimed not simply at making life easier, but rather at indulging the slothful.

Automobiles, drive-ins, remote controls, voice-activated devices. Push-buttons instead of toggle switches. Electric can-openers in place of hand operated ones. Escalators, elevators and moving ramps as a substitute for stairs.

Alas, I could go on and on as the list of convenience products commonly available during *The Decline* is endless.

Even the law in that crazy time was complicit. One in particular mandated replacing all door knobs with handles that were easier to manipulate.

And consumers completely bought into this insanity, purchasing all those novel, labour-saving items as soon as they were advertised.

Unsurprisingly, this resulted in a glut of surplus junk and

a crushing mass of garbage that desecrated our planet and was a major contributor to *The Final Catastrophe*.

And as hard as it is to believe today, during *The Decline* many people bragged about how easily they could live fully functional lives without ever leaving their dwelling places. How they could, in fact, purchase all manner of goods, food and entertainment online from the comfort of their homes.

The absurdity of it all. All those ruined lives for the sake of the god of expediency. No wonder the crime of Sloth escalated beyond all others.

On a much more positive note, let me remind you how the United Entities of the World is working to put an end to this criminal behaviour.

Most obviously, we have instituted mandatory tracking of activities and enforced fitness benchmarks and goals to ensure that everyone in our society keeps physically active.

As you know, we are all required to log our 10,000 steps and attend obligatory exercise sessions every day.

All of us must unconditionally meet our health targets or face the consequences.

And there are penalties for those who do not comply.

Hefty fines and compulsory boot camps are just a few of the primary punishments imposed under *The Health and Well-Being Act*.

And although these rules and regulations are imperative, the corrective remedy for Sloth goes far beyond the physical requirements.

Living rationally with a sense of purpose is realistically the only cure for this miserable crime.

And that's why the UEW has enshrined the obligation to live a meaningful life not only into *The Global Human Rights Code,* but also into our *Law of Commitments*.

Sheri Does the Inventory Her Way!

Let me tell you more about my Mdina glass and how I came to acquire it for that also has to do with the creation of life.

My husband and I had been visiting Sicily, tramping along with throngs of tourists through the Greek ruins in Agrigento. I was feeling a little nauseous from the heat of the day and the crowds, so we settled down on a stone bench under an archway out of the broiling sun.

An Australian couple about our age, taking a break from the tour as well, spoke passionately about the megalithic temples, some of the oldest free-standing structures in the world, on Malta.

They raved about the island's history and the fact that it was unsullied by commercial tourism. Best of all, it was just a short ferry ride away.

On the spur of the moment we were sailing to Valletta, the capital of Malta. I do find that most good things happen spontaneously, don't you?

And we did have a wonderful time exploring not just the prehistoric monuments, but also the town of Mdina. I recall being enchanted by its medieval quarter perched on a rocky promontory above the sea, and absolutely captivated by its beautiful glass art.

We booked a personal tour of the glass workshop, talked to several of the glass-blowers plying their ancient craft and ended up ogling row after row of dazzling masterpieces in the gift shop.

I looked at my husband's azure blue eyes, thought of the Mediterranean and bought the striking piece that sits in our kitchen to this day.

It was only after we got home that I found out that I was

pregnant with Karen. The queasiness that I had felt on Sicily was morning sickness.

For that reason, the Mdina glass that I so greatly value will always remind me of my daughter and that sacred time when I was full of life and happy expectations.

Museum of the Obsolete - Tobacco

For centuries people ignited tobacco leaves and inhaled its smoke for relaxation. At first they burned tobacco in pipes, but by the 20th century, cigarettes, small, paper-wrapped rolls filled with finely cut leaves, were the most commonly used method for inhaling the vapours.

Smoking cigarettes peaked in the 1960s before the health hazards and addictiveness of this recreation became well known. Subsequently, second hand smoke also proved to be toxic and by the Millennium, many governments had banned smoking in both public and corporate facilities.

Even though smoking became more and more socially unacceptable during *The Decline* era, manufacturing these cancer sticks had still grown into a $35 billion business, responsible for eight million deaths a year worldwide.

This was due to their highly addictive properties and to the tobacco industry's intensive marketing and extensive advertising specifically aimed at young people who had not yet formed a dependency.

During *The Great Resolve*, the United Entities of the World prohibited the planting and growing of tobacco and the production of cigarettes.

Drafters of these laws cited not only the health risks connected with this vile habit, but also the waste of resources used in their cultivation, manufacture and distribution.

Qs & As from the Clutter-Buster's Blog

Dear Clutter-Buster:

I'd always thought that I had a good relationship with my mother and my younger sister. But now I find that the two of them have been doing things behind my back that are most upsetting.

My mom recently gave my sister the cookbook that my great-grandmother had put together, as well as the family photo album also dating from that time.

And she never even asked me if I wanted them or if I had room for them in my allotment.

I know she did this because I saw a copy of the Passing-On Allowance form on her tab when I was using it to look up a book title. What should I do? - *fretting and festering*

Dear Fretting and Festering:

"Mom always loved you best" was a gag line in the Smothers Brothers comedy show in the mid-years of the last century. Unfortunately, it's a truism that underlies a great deal of family strife.

However, passing on two items to your younger sister does not prove that your mother likes her better than you or that there is a conspiracy against you.

Your sister may have asked for the cookbook and photo album. And your mother may have given in to her desires, not knowing that you had any interest in them.

Instead of fretting, I suggest that you talk calmly to your mom about your feelings. Perhaps over a lovely lunch - your treat of course.

Yes, it may be hard to share your jealous thoughts even with your mother, especially if you've not lived at home for a while. But I think it best to do so now, before she passes on more stuff that you might like.

Bring lots of tissue and be prepared for a few tears to be shed as you make things right between you again.

A Chorus of Voices
Jim Discovers His Mom Had Closets

Hi Steve, I thought that your followers with elderly parents might want to take a closer look at how they're managing. I sure wish I had asked more questions. Here's the scoop.

I recently went to empty my mother's apartment after she passed and I couldn't believe what I found - un-boarded up closets in her bedroom, in the hallway and even in the guest room. Not only that, but they were what used to be called walk-in closets.

And they were jam-packed with boxes heaped on top of boxes and tons of clothes hung helter-skelter. Plus dozens of shoes, boots, sandals and slippers - both hers and my late father's - were jumbled on the floor between the cartons.

God knows what's inside the boxes. I'm afraid to open them. So I definitely can't fill out the Inventory of Items for Disposal on Death form. That's where you have to list all the things that she hadn't gotten rid of before her death. And I'm supposed to submit the Final Exit form in the next five days.

I know I should calm down, and yeah, I'm sure this must happen lots of time with people who already had too much stuff when the law came into effect.

So I expect that I'm not alone here. But Steve, I'm in shock. I never expected this. She never let on, not even at the end. It's so freaking embarrassing.

Laszlo the Fixer

Did you feel vindicated after The Final Catastrophe?

In a small way. Except the years leading up to *The Decline* were so dismal that it was hard to feel good about being validated as a prophet of doom.

It was more that you could see humanity heading for disaster and you felt damn frustrated and incredibly helpless.

Our tiny community of Fixers couldn't do bugger all, just hunker down and wait.

We actually had no impact; we were so puny, just a speck in the sandstorm that was engulfing the world.

You became a hero though, winning the Citizen's Medal for your contribution to The Great Resolve.

Yeah, I had my moment of glory. Ten minutes of fame.

But crap, I only did what was called for, helped where I could. Rallied the community of Fixers to come out of the wood-work and move into the political arena.

It kind of went against the grain for most of us though. However, it was a time of desperate need and we stepped up to do our bit.

We were, and I emphasize it wasn't me alone, all of us together were able to help lay the foundation for the anti-consumer society that came into being after *The Final Catastrophe.* We could draw not only on our skills as Fixers, but also on our collective experience of thriving with less.

And last year you won the Nu-Nobel Prize for Humanity. How does that feel?

I was dumbfounded. Still am.

While pleased and honoured, I sincerely feel that there are a lot more worthy recipients who the UEW could have honoured in this way.

Young people who are making such a difference now. People like Phoebe Alicana, Byron Fields, Jake Juneja. So many more deserving than me. I'm sure, Steve, that you could name quite a few yourself.

I've kind of had my life. My achievements are all behind me. It's better to give a break to those who can benefit from the accolades.

Sheri Does the Inventory Her Way!

Even though it's just an object, I always felt there was something sacred - and profane - about the Crown Ducal ceramic bowl that's the next item on my personal inventory.

How can anything so delicate have survived for more than a century?

This jewel of lustreware, created in 1920, features four exquisite butterflies painted in opalescent mother-of-pearl. Adding to its sublime beauty was the fact that it was a gift from my older sister, Lena.

A truly generous present because she really loved that magnificent piece and I'm sure found it hard to part with. Yet once she saw how I admired it in its revered place above her fireplace, she insisted that I take it home with me.

Now every time I look at it, the memory of Lena and her kind-heartedness sanctifies it. And I can't help but sense that the bowl holds her benevolent spirit as well.

The divine vessel also contains the spirit of butterflies, those iconic symbols of transformation. Their miraculous metamorphosis from egg to caterpillar to chrysalis to flying insect mirrors the marvellous stages of growth and change in our lives.

Still, there's also something sad about the butterflies on that bowl. When I look at them, I can't help but see the now extinct Monarchs - those majestic creatures whose celebrated annual migrations from Canada to Mexico tragically ended during *The Decline*.

And I regret that people didn't take action as the number of butterflies and other insects decreased in the early years of the Millennium.

Instead, we ignored their peril as we disregarded so many of nature's warnings over the years. Sadly, most of us failed to see that the demise of the Monarchs was a portent of the dire consequences of society's selfish preoccupation with acquiring more and more.

Industrial overplanting of corn crops and sterilizing the agricultural landscape with pesticides to increase yields wiped out millions of acres of native plants including milkweed, the vital source of nectar for Monarch larvae.

By turning fertile farm lands over to corporations whose goal was productivity above all else, we created vast waste lands and biological deserts.

Natural habitats disappeared and that loss reverberated throughout the insect and bird world, and right on up the food chain.

We had, for sure, drowned paradise with pesticides.

So I appreciate the paradox of life made visible in my butterfly bowl.

And I have a fresh understanding of how the sacred and the profane can co-exist in one precious object.

The Seven Crimes of Consumerism

My fellow colleagues, this brings us to the last of the seven crimes of consumerism and that is the dastardly Wrath.

Of all the offences that I've outlined for you, this felony is the one that most often leads to physical violence and because of this, it has the most visible victims.

Legally, Wrath is defined as inappropriate anger and hatred directed outwards.

It includes vicious actions undertaken because of revenge or the desire for punitive measures outside of courts of law.

In the unrestrained frenzy of rage anything can, and often does, happen. More killings and property destruction occur because of this one serious crime than through all the other crimes combined.

But what you may not realize is that anger is intimately connected to consumerism and also to the laws created to prevent overconsumption.

For this reason, I'll provide you with a few examples of how the crime of Wrath is most commonly manifested in our society today.

People regularly get furious because they've reached their quota in some category of consumer goods. They rant and rave when they can't add something to *The Grand Inventory* that they feel is their due.

They even become incensed when they are asked to fill out an exemption form as required by law.

Many become irrational when asked to provide their allotment number, spouting verbal abuse not only at the law, but also at the hard-working public servants interpreting the rules for them.

I'm sure that most of you are familiar with the many

methods that we have developed to punish these criminals and the severe sentences that we impose upon conviction.

What you may not be aware of are the numerous new rehabilitation treatments that we recently added to our already large arsenal of effective programs.

These include compulsory anger management training, mandatory tai-chi and yoga sessions, hypnosis, silent retreats and forced meditations. All part of our effort to prevent these irate law-breakers from recidivism.

That being said, I must remind you that all the seven toxic crimes of consumerism that I've been reviewing for you today, overlap and feed off each other.

And when you have an entire community filled with these criminals, then you have a consumer-oriented society headed for another catastrophe.

Thus, we must be vigilant in our eradication of these seven deadly offences. We must ensure that such an out-of-control culture does not ever happen again.

And we must make certain that the perpetrators of any of these heinous crimes are not only swiftly caught, but also appropriately punished.

Museum of the Obsolete - Newspapers

Throughout the 19th and 20th centuries, the most prevalent informational media was the newspaper.

Newspapers were paper-based, printed publications that reported current events and contained commentaries and articles on a broad range of topics.

These mass communication vehicles were delivered to people's homes and workplaces daily by subscription. Individual copies were also for sale in kiosks and in stores.

Even though the time-consuming manufacturing process involved in publishing the papers made the news out-of-date by the time people received them, the newspaper industry prospered. It reached an astounding $60 billion peak at the start of the Millennium.

However by that point too, the industry was destroying four billion trees annually. And people were increasingly receiving instantaneous, up-to-the-minute information and news 24/7 from more ecological media including television, radio and the Internet.

This paradigm shift ultimately led to the cessation of newspaper publishing during *The Decline* and the concurrent conservation of trees, water and other valuable resources that had been used to produce and distribute these antiquated methods of communication.

Qs & As from the Clutter-Buster's Blog

Dear Clutter-Buster:

I am a veterinarian. An elderly client recently carried in her calico cat for treatment of a urinary infection. A week later, she brought in a tabby to check for ear mites.

She told me that the tabby belonged to her son, but I suspect that it was hers. I had always thought that she was a spinster and she had never mentioned a son.

Do I report her for exceeding *The One Pet per Person per Household Law* or respect her story? She is quite old and I know how attached the aged can be to their pets. I don't want to cause her undue distress. - *confused doc*

Dear Confused Doc:

I hear your compassion and feel your concern about this

lady. However, as you know from the DSM, hoarding is a recognized mental illness.

And vets are often the first to notice signs of this disorder when owners seek help for a steady stream of sick or injured animals. You may have only seen two cats up to now, but you should be aware that people with this disease may accumulate dozens or even hundreds of pets.

The animals may be confined inside the house, so that they can be concealed more easily. And unfortunately too, because of their sheer numbers, these creatures often aren't cared for properly.

Ethically and professionally, I urge you to report your client, so that her compulsion can be treated appropriately.

Random Notes on *The Decline*
Paving over Paradise

More offbeat history as Xavier Sansun submits an essay on storage to In the Middle of Things.

No blogsters, not data, software, memory or cloud storage. But rather the more concrete, physical warehousing concept that goes back to mankind's earliest history.

Read on, and you'll find out why The Great Resolve banned all private storage areas.

My thesis is that the unparalleled proliferation of storage sites for personal property and for private vehicles played a crucial role in *The Decline* and was a major contributor to *The Final Catastrophe*.

I believe that one of the primary reasons for this was the change in the function of storage areas from commercial way-stations for the temporary warehousing of commodities to private facilities for storing personal belongings for an indeterminate length of time.

Greek, Roman, Egyptian and Chinese historical accounts, all make reference to storehouses for the provisional safe-guarding of grains, wine, and merchandise for trade. And archaeological sites around the world show evidence of institutional buildings that were specifically used as interim holding areas.

Starting in the 19th century and continuing well into the Millennium, department stores - which incidentally had a key role to play in the rise of consumerism - were also used to keep goods for the short-term until they were sold.

During *The Decline* however, storage took on a new role that was so weird as to be perverse.

Storage became defined as a space where people stowed their excess possessions indefinitely.

The need for using storage spaces in this way was a direct result of the 20th century's mushrooming consumer society and the unparalleled rise of suburbia.

This immense expansion of the outlying areas of cities encouraged gross materialism, rampant overconsumption, devastating waste, an overwhelming car culture, and the need for massive amounts of storage space.

People didn't just build ordinary houses in the suburbs. Rather they erected mega-dwellings so gigantic that they required enormous amounts of labour and energy both to construct and to maintain.

And these houses contained far more rooms than any person or family needed to live comfortably and contentedly.

To fill up the rooms in their mega-homes and to preserve their status, people coveted and purchased more and more things. Soon enough, they found that they had far more goods than they could readily make use of.

And when their room-sized closets were packed beyond capacity with household and personal items, then empty rooms, basements and garages became additional places for stashing the excess.

These mansions were, of course, the result of insatiable greed and overweening pride.

Despite the glut of items and the lack of storage space in and around their homes, the mega-dwellers relentlessly continued to buy more and more stuff that they didn't need.

It was no surprise then that before long people were paying their hard-earned dollars to rent holding pens for things that they had absolutely no use for. And so facilities for hoarding useless personal goods grew exponentially.

Commercial storage compounds first appeared in the United States in 1958. These businesses rented out rooms, lockers, containers, and outdoor areas for the superfluous. And they thrived.

Self-storage reached its zenith during *The Decline* when more than a hundred thousand facilities covered millions of acres worldwide.

Yes, most reprehensibly, the world's invaluable land resources were senselessly wasted in order to harbour mega-tonnes of worthless junk.

As an aside, self-storage is an interesting term.

It's as if people's relationship to their belongings was so intimate that they were putting themselves away. And perhaps, they truly were locking up their very souls in these storage facilities.

Suburbanites also had an intense connection to another of their possessions that was essential to their lifestyle and that required colossal amounts of storage space when not in use: their automobiles.

Deplorably, people, especially those living in suburbia, were not satisfied with owning just a single car. They had to have two, three or four vehicles - seemingly one for every member of their family.

And when idle, these billions of motor vehicles needed to be stored somewhere.

So in fact a good portion of housing development areas was given over to driveways and multi-vehicle garages. As well, parking lots engulfed miles and miles of prime land both in cities and in suburbs.

Inconceivably too, entire lanes of public thoroughfares were also used for storing automobiles. This obscenity was known as on-street parking.

We could laugh at the ridiculousness of it all and wonder how the situation could have gotten so outlandish. But the real tragedy was that in a world and a time that we no longer know, vast areas of our fertile earth were made fallow, so that thoughtless and inconsiderate people could cling to their totally useless goods and chattels in perpetuity.

Amy Speaks
How to Live your Life with Space to Spare

Let me tell you about *The Clutter-Buster's Manifesto* - my philosophy of de-cluttering that outlines ten principles for divesting yourself and your environment of the encumbrance of things.

And let me assure you that if you keep to these standards, you will lead a wonderful life with loads of space to spare.

As I mentioned earlier, my goal was to limit these precepts to ten simple rules.

So here they are:

1. Adhere to *The Naked Law - Naked you came into this world, naked you must leave it*. This is the supreme code of the civilized world and the basis for living in a clutter-free state. Everything follows from this primary law.

2. Stick to the limits of *The Grand Inventory*. Add to your allotment with the end of your life in mind. If you put something in, take something out. Avoid exemptions.

3. Eliminate everything but the essential. Identify what is important and get rid of everything else. Downsize. Reduce your possessions to the bare minimum. Repeat the mantra: *I have enough, I do enough, I am enough*. Remember that empty is good, full is bad.

4. Use what you have. Be satisfied with what you own rather than craving more or different things. Remember there is beauty and comfort in your old and worn possessions. Don't replace them with new items.

5. Don't buy something unless it's absolutely necessary. Build your resistance muscle.

6. Forego gifting of material things. Instead, give others the intangible gifts of your time and your attention.

7. Practise self-sufficiency. Limit your dependency on mechanical and technological devices.

8. Edit your life and work commitments. Do away with multi-tasking. Be mindful. Maintain a work-life balance by respecting your life energy.

9. Put everything in its proper place. Set up and maintain organizational systems in order to save time and to minimize stress as much as possible.

10. Take a communal approach to life. Share with others.

Sheri Does the Inventory Her Way!

The overplanting of corn may have caused the destruction of milkweed and the Monarch butterfly; however, this hardy vegetable was once revered for its sustenance and treated like a deity in a culture and a time far removed from ours.

Maize was the cornerstone of the Mayan civilization. And each stage in its planting was preceded by elaborate religious rituals - a far cry from the immense industrialized growing methods predominant during *The Decline*.

And for me, nothing portrays the blessedness of that food staple more than the large clay statue of a maize god, the only keepsake except for memories, that I carried back from our first visit to Mexico City.

My husband and I had been working flat out for several months and desperately needed a break.

Christmas season was upon us and we longed to flee from the social obligations and forced bonhomie of that time of year. We craved sunshine, but not beaches and wanted a locale not too far from home. And as both of us were interested in archaeology, we wanted to visit some ruins, museums and art galleries on our vacation.

So when I came across a good deal on a flight and a hotel in the historic centre of Mexico City, it was a no-brainer.

Our week in that vast metropolis was filled with strange vignettes. Some were delightful like the fully decked out Santa sitting astride a deer-drawn sleigh in the tropical heat while palm trees swayed in the background. Santa shook his sleigh bells gleefully as two buxom women climbed into his cushiony lap.

Nearby, multi-coloured flashing lights lit up a life-size *crèche* featuring the Jesus-Mary-Joseph trio with their customary entourage. People strolled arm-in-arm in the sunshine eating ice cream and had their shoes polished at kiosks decorated with tinsel.

Even the regal statue of Beethoven in the park near our hotel sported a jaunty Santa cap.

Other more disturbing scenes revealed abject poverty and the callousness of people. A skinny little girl with her hand outstretched shyly approached stranger after stranger as her father played raucous carols on his time-worn accordion. Not one in twenty gave her a coin and still she persisted.

A small street urchin, wearing a dirty and torn t-shirt and sockless tattered shoes, quietly smiled as he read a comic book while his pitiful array of votive candles were laid out for sale on the ground beside him.

A woman in rags clutched a newborn to her breast on the steps of a cathedral as pious church-goers passed her by without a glance.

Consequently, I found myself marvelling at the glorious, gold-encrusted cathedrals, but at the same time I was also perplexed by the shameful neglect outside the doors. In the marketplace, I was alternately amused by the madcap festive icons to death and strangely moved to tears by the garish religious relics.

Indeed, the full panoply of life with its peculiar blend of sacredness and the profane somehow seemed close to the surface and more visible here.

In a busy craft market, we came across a pottery stall that displayed a huge assortment of genial clay gods and goddesses. And I couldn't help but think how different they were from the harsh, autocratic Christian deity from the *Book of Job* who would tolerate no idols.

So I chose for my memento of Mexico City, a two-foot

high figure resplendent in his corn-row head-dress and his beatific smiling face. I hoped when we carried our maize idol home that his nurturing spirit would spread throughout our household.

He now stands with his feet firmly planted next to the fireplace in our living room. His fists clutch not weapons of destruction, but two stalks of life-giving maize.

And as I add him to my unique inventory, I realize that his serene countenance has definitely given me many years of nourishing contentment.

I think that over time the objects that we chance upon and then decide to possess and treasure reflect not only our feelings and our desires, but also our very souls.

Museum of the Obsolete - Film Cameras

From the mid-1800s and continuing into the Millennium, cameras used film, a light sensitive medium, to produce photographs.

Film was costly and processing it into viewable pictures was a lengthy procedure. And as film cameras did not have viewing screens, people would have to wait until the film was developed to see what their photos looked like.

The chemicals used in processing and developing film were highly toxic and they also depleted massive amounts of irreplaceable natural resources.

What's more, these one-purpose, picture-making devices were extremely limited in scope. They could neither store images nor transfer them to computers.

So during *The Decline,* the production of film cameras came to an end and they were completely replaced by digital cameras and image recorders built into other equipment.

Qs & As from the Clutter-Buster's Blog

Dear Clutter-Buster:

I am a new grandmother and knitted a blanket for my first grandchild. When I went to give them my present, my son and his wife told me that they already had their quota of blankets and refused to accept it.

I'm so upset and I really don't know what to do.

It's quite spoiled any joy that I have in celebrating my grandson's birth. - *unravelling granny*

Dear Unravelling Granny:

Congratulations on becoming a grandma for the first time! While your heart is in the right place, your values have somehow gotten stuck in DTD - during *The Decline*.

You need to buy into the precepts of *The Great Resolve* to ensure that your grandchild continues to grow up in a society liberated from overconsumption and free of the greed and lust that can develop for unnecessary things.

I'm sorry to tell you, but as your son and daughter-in-law already have maxed out their allowance, you have no choice, but to start unravelling the blanket now. Go granny go!

A Chorus of Voices
The Reinvention of Betsy LaVie

Once *The Naked Law* came into effect, everyone struggled to fill out the mandatory inventory form and get rid of their useless possessions. And as you would expect, the definition of useless varied greatly.

Owners of art and antiques were in the forefront of those

clamouring for exceptions. They thought of themselves as connoisseurs rather than as mere consumers.

Under the law though, antiquity, rareness, and beauty were all meaningless attributes. To get an exemption, you needed to provide solid reasons for keeping an object or holding on to a collection.

Succinct rationales attached to the Declaration of Worth and Value for Artefacts and the Statement of Essentiality forms largely determined whether you could retain your belongings, or not.

As you can well imagine, there were big bucks for writers of these justification reports. Former advertising copywriters were in great demand and widely available since most were unemployed after the outright banning of all marketing for consumer products.

In fact, after *The Great Resolve* anyone in promotion and publicity was considered a pariah. They were looked down upon as major contributors to the epidemic of excessiveness so inherent in society during *The Decline*.

A few of them reinvented themselves as government communicators. Yet after a career of spouting hype, they found it almost impossible to write the simple and clear information mandated by law.

However writing expressive and gushy rationales was right up their alley. Positioning an item's intangible value was their forte. And none was better at it than Betsy LaVie.

Betsy went from being an award-winning producer of pharmaceutical ads - you may remember the commercials for Extolite and EnhanceMent, both her babies - to crafting convincing justifications for the collections of some of the largest museums in the world.

Word had it that she had a team of editors who parsed

and trimmed all her writing to get to the required level of clarity. And she hired a group of researchers to analyse the readability of each word and assess its persuasiveness rating.

Here's Betsy's terse, but successful, forty-word rationale for keeping the collection intact at the Warhol museum:

"Andy Warhol, master of reproduction art in mid-20th century America, depicted the out-of-control, profligate consumer society and the wild celebrity-mania of that time. His superficial works trace commercialism during *The Decline*, inadvertently proving the absolute necessity for *The Naked Law*."

But what could ordinary folk do?

The Museums of Non-Essential Goods that were set up in each city were overwhelmed with people donating their valued possessions all at once.

Soon they put restrictions in place and rigidly enforced *The Noah's Ark Limitation* - two-of-everything, first-come, first-accepted. Value judgements were non-existent.

If a museum had two model cars, it wouldn't take yours. Even if it was a titanium replica of a Maserati and what the museum had were made in Taiwan plastic giveaways.

Rarity, uniqueness, monetary or aesthetic worth - those now forgotten attributes of the art world - lost all meaning and all significance, instantly rendering precious objects non-essential and redundant.

Laszlo the Fixer

And one last question, Laszlo. Is there anything that you've encountered that can't be fixed?

Yeah Steve, a lot of the stuff produced during *The Decline* in what used to be called the Third World. Sub-standard in the first place, not worth repairing.

And plastics. For sure, there are no artisans of synthetics. Although I do recall that when 3D printers were introduced, they were marketed to artists. Create plastic models easily and cheaply. But really, who needs more machine-made, imitation junk.

Plastics are the worst and the new admin is still tackling the enormous problem of disposing of these things. Broken or not, they last forever. They're chemically inert, so they never disintegrate. And you can't incinerate them without causing lethal toxins.

In actual fact, the world before *The Final Catastrophe* produced so much artificial crap that you couldn't bury it all, even if you dug up the whole earth.

But anything that was made well in the first place can be fixed. You can either do it yourself with the help of All-Tube videos. Or you can Search-All and find someone who will gladly do it for you.

Your followers might want to check out the collective's website - thefixers.uew or findafixer.uew where you can post whatever it is that you need revamped and people will bid on restoring it for you.

Every worker registered with those sites is a professional and the jobs come with reliability pledges. Read a few of the testimonials from real people who you can link to. No anon heads allowed.

Thank you, Laszlo.

For background information and a history of the Fixers, you might want to check out their Megapedia entry; also these popular bestsellers all available on Amazoogle:

A Concise and Unabridged History of the Fixers
by J. J. Smithy;
An Examination and Analysis of the First Rebels against Overconsumption by Cindy Rollick;
Fixing the Mess and Other Tales from the Frontlines of a Broken Society by Amanda P. Watson;
Fixing What's Wrong with Society by Flux;
How I Turned My Back on Corporate Life and Learned to Love Simplicity by Helmut Schluss;
How the Fixers Helped Society Mend by Sofia Zizzo;
How the Fixers Saved Society from Overconsumption by George Imany and Patrick Dale;
Making Things Work Again: Tales of a Broken Life by Derek B. Riley;
Mend, Repair, Fix by Sally Bird;
My Life as an Itinerant Fixer, a Personal Reminiscence by Edith Hedi;
Patch It: A New Psychology of Living by Fred Cannon;
The Last of a Breed: True Tales from Yesterday by Steve Discony;
Underground with the Fixers by Triumph Spinoza;
View from the Other Side of More by Less;
Who Are You Going To Call? by William Golightly.

Sheri Does the Inventory Her Way!

The descriptions of the items on my personal inventory may lead you to think that I only yearned for and acquired rather frivolous, impractical objects. Things which I surely could have lived without.

However that was not the case. Let me tell you the story of a practical item that's still very much in use in my kitchen today. It is a heavy aluminum pot with a tight-fitting lid, long past its original function as a pressure cooker.

If I remember correctly when I bought this pot at an estate auction along with a carton full of other cookware, it had a pressure regulator. But as it was old and came without instructions, I worried that it might explode and so never used it that way.

Nevertheless, I did use it constantly.

And over time, that bargain pot became my favourite for cooking staples such as porridge, rice and stew. Anything really that required simmering for a long time in a sturdy, thick-bottomed container.

Believe it or not, through all its re-purposed existence, it has not tarnished or shown signs of wear.

To be sure, the rubber ring gasket on the lid rotted away a long time ago, but the flanged lid lock still provides an excellent seal when needed.

I wish I could say the same for my other pots and pans with their easy-to-scratch, non-stick coatings or their easy-to-warp, thin metal castings.

I won't tell you how many of them were discarded over the years, or how often I fretted about the toxicity of the materials they were made from. Not to mention the waste of money on all those costly cast-offs.

Yes, this sturdy pot has accompanied me on my culinary adventures for the past forty years. And to think that I bid only two dollars and won an entire lot of metal-ware and assorted utensils along with it.

I dare say that winning that bargain box of goodies certainly contributed greatly to my enduring passion for, and enthusiastic participation in, auctions.

As a matter of fact, auctions actually became our default

store for household purchases. And a quick tour of our house today would show you that a good ninety percent of our possessions came from them, along with rummage sales and used goods stores.

My husband and I truly embraced a conservation-oriented lifestyle decades before the Magic Nine was even dreamt of.

I imagine that if more people had followed the precepts of the 3 Rs, lived simply and bought second-hand, *The Final Catastrophe* could have been prevented, or at the very least postponed.

I expect though that's more than likely just wishful thinking. For even with the ever increasing distress signals during *The Decline*, the majority of people continued to revel in their conspicuous consumption habit and strove relentlessly not just to keep up with their neighbours, but to surpass them.

Disappointingly, even *The Final Catastrophe* failed to shift the core assumptions of many people about what makes for a good life. While the laws created by *The Great Resolve* forced behavioural changes, I don't think that they altered society's collective consciousness one iota.

And if directives against overindulgence and squandering resources didn't exist, I fear that far too many people would revert to how they lived during *The Decline*.

I truly believe that the only hope for real systemic change lies with the young generation who has known no other way of life than that dictated by *The Great Resolve*.

Even though I balk at some of the restrictions and stupid ordinances of the law, like the damn inventory form, I am genuinely pleased that the new regime's philosophy is grounded in the attributes of Reduce, Reuse, Recycle, and the principles of the entire simple living movement.

Museum of the Obsolete - Mail

Prior to email and instant messaging, people communicated in written form by sending paper documents through a government-operated organization called the postal system. This non-virtual transmission method was known as mail.

To use the mail service, senders would put their letters, cards, bill payments and other documents into envelopes addressed to recipients and physically deposit them in mail boxes or at special posting offices for delivery locally and around the world. Payment for this service was in the form of government issued postage stamps - small adhesive bits of paper that senders bought and affixed to the envelopes.

The postal system used numerous transportation vehicles including trucks, trains, boats and airplanes to get mail to its destination. The process ended with a human letter-carrier personally delivering the mail directly to the addressee's home or office.

This procedure could take days or even weeks depending on the distance between sender and recipient. And once computer-generated correspondence become common, this slow, highly labour intensive and costly dispatch mechanism became known derisively as "snail mail."

During *The Decline,* cyber-communications completely replaced paper-based mail, putting an end to all government postal systems.

Qs & As from the Clutter-Buster's Blog

Dear Clutter-Buster:
I am asking this question about a friend of mine. She and

her husband want to get a divorce, so that they can double the number of household possessions that they are allowed to own. They plan, however, to continue to live together and to keep all their conjugal ties intact after the divorce.

This bothers me terribly and I wonder if I should continue my relationship with her. What do you think? - *perturbed*

Dear Perturbed:

While what they are doing is legal, I think it is unethical and surely does not comply with the intent or the spirit of *The Naked Law*.

You have a right to speak your mind, but be prepared to see the friendship fizzle. Up to now, you have been chums, but you have learned something about your friend's ethics that cannot be ignored. People who do not share the same values rarely remain close.

The Seven Crimes of Consumerism

I promised in my opening remarks that I would give you one comprehensive example of an object that neatly encapsulated the very essence of the seven crimes of consumerism. This was something so ubiquitous during *The Decline* that many people believe that it alone led to *The Final Catastrophe*.

This formerly progressive and innovative manufactured product not only outlived its usefulness, but also caused devastating global damage on a mind-boggling scale.

It was that now generally shunned, motorized vehicle, the automobile.

Unfortunately, the proclivity for committing three core offences - Envy, Pride and Lust - was built in to automobile ownership from early on.

This was because most people coveted cars not for their practicality or efficiency, but rather for such superficialities as brand name and costliness.

People yearned incessantly for cutting edge, state-of-the-art, luxury vehicles. And competitive jealousy about cars led all too frequently to the crimes associated with hatred, lying and stealing.

Furthermore, many people so utterly identified with their automobiles that they completely failed to see that having a car was more of a cause for embarrassment and for shame, than for glee.

Car owners should have felt mortified by their vehicles' detrimental effect both on health and on the environment. Yet oblivious to the inanity of their lifestyle, far too many drivers disdained eco-friendly mass transit and openly sneered at those who used it.

It's hard to imagine today that citizens wilfully ignored the vileness inherent in these grown-up toys. And instead spent their lives working to buy and to constantly upgrade to more extravagant models that were only cosmetically better than their still serviceable, current vehicles.

Such unbridled Lust for the new resulted in severe debt and outright bankruptcy as the purchase and maintenance of cars were major, recurrent, non-tax deductible expenditures.

And most deplorably, the automotive industry was totally complicit in fostering these crimes.

The most expensive advertising campaigns in the history of the world made it next to impossible for people to resist their influence.

In fact, marketing costs for motor vehicles far outpaced the era's other mega-spenders - pharmaceuticals, financials and media outlets.

During *The Decline,* car companies spent over $20 billion annually to promote their products. That's $20 billion not to manufacture automobiles, but just to spread Lust and Greed for them.

And consumers readily bought in to the erroneous belief that everyone deserved a car of their own. Instead of sharing a vehicle, every household that could afford it, and many that could not, greedily purchased separate cars for each and every family member of driving age.

Not only that, but many people self-indulgently owned more than one car for themselves.

These pricey and totally unnecessary extra autos were viewed as valid perks of success. Supposedly exemplifying the good life, they ranged from sports and racing cars to huge SUVs, trucks and vintage automobiles.

And absurdly too, such automotive excesses were seldom taken out on the road because, obviously, one person could only drive one vehicle at a time.

Exemplars of Greed indeed!

We know now that this wasteful product led to a society of car-people who venerated the crime of Sloth.

Certainly, the very act of owning an automobile seemed to breed laziness in people.

Instead of walking, seemingly everyone drove to their corner store. Even more disconcertingly, they chauffeured their children to schools and daycares that were only blocks away from their homes.

Naturally, most commercial conglomerates supported and definitely encouraged this indolent lifestyle. Fast-food restaurants, banks and pharmacies all promoted a convenient drive-through option, so people no longer had to get out of their vehicles and walk into a building to buy something.

These caraholics were also selfishly unconcerned that the emissions from enormous numbers of idling cars at drive-through businesses considerably increased air pollution.

Because of their deliberate slothfulness, much of the populace eventually found themselves unable to walk even short distances.

And not surprisingly, this lazy automobile-based way of life directly contributed to the unprecedented increase in obesity rates that reached near epidemic levels globally during *The Decline*.

We, today, are still dealing with the fallout from the car culture of that unenlightened time. Lamentably, obesity, along with diabetes, heart disease, disability and premature death remain prevalent in our society.

And they are just a sampling of the automobile's long-term devastating effects on human health.

The last of the seven deadly offences that I will discuss in connection to motor vehicles is undeniably a horrendous one. It is the felony of Wrath.

In looking back, we can now see clearly that people driving automobiles were more often than not bursting with pent-up anger and aggression.

Truly, it seems as if the very act of getting behind the wheel in a car transformed otherwise polite and reasonable citizens into enraged lawbreakers.

The laws that these miscreants violated ranged from minor infractions such as parking in prohibited zones to major criminal acts such as hit and runs.

And as you may already know, the unmanageable Wrath of car drivers also spawned a pervasive, deadly menace known as road rage.

In actual fact, this outrageous fury, with its disastrous

consequences, was so commonplace during *The Decline* as to become virtually unremarkable.

Because of this, we have, unfortunately, no way to fully tally the statistics on the number of accidents and lives lost to this contemptible scourge, although we do know that it was substantial.

So there you have it - Envy, Pride, Lust, Greed, Sloth and Wrath - six of the quintessential crimes of consumerism intrinsic to one loathsome product - the automobile.

And we are indeed fortunate in this enlightened time that *The Great Resolve* regulated and severely restricted the use of these reprehensible monsters of consumerism.

News Watch

Breaking news from the United Entities of the World: King Harry offloads Balmoral Castle and Sandringham House to share royal riches with the poor.

Following in the footsteps of Saint Frank who dismantled the Vatican's vast holdings to help the needy, King Harry is selling off the British Crown's private holdings in order to disburse an estimated $50 million to charitable organizations that work with the destitute.

In making the surprise announcement, King Harry said, "*The Final Catastrophe* has caused me to re-examine the role the British monarchy should play in the new society.

"I believe in carrying on the tradition of the monarchy as a figurehead with all its ceremonial functions, but that role does not require holding on to immense, unused assets. I did nothing to earn this wealth and I feel strongly that it belongs to the people.

"I have therefore set the wheels in motion to distribute

these ancient assets to impoverished people everywhere."

Although the names of the charities to benefit are still to be determined, it is expected that they will be worldwide humanitarian aid groups, not limited to Britain.

King Harry cannot dispose of the Crown estate properties held in trust for the nation or his successors that are worth an estimated $10 billion. These include Buckingham Palace, Windsor Castle, the Crown Jewels and the Royal Collection.

However in making the announcement about his private holdings, King Harry said that he was also officially asking the United Entities of the World to pass an Act to take over the British Crown properties held in trusts in order to dispose of them and to distribute the proceeds to the indigent.

Commentators lauded King Harry's decision calling it "unprecedented," "a truly altruistic act," and "deserving of sainthood." Many noted that the King's mother, the late Princess Diana, known as the People's Princess, would have been immensely proud of his selfless action.

Amy Speaks
How to Live your Life with Space to Spare

Before opening the floor to questions, I want to give you all a few practical tips so that when you leave here, you can dive right in to freeing your home from clutter.

These pointers are from the chapter on de-cluttering in my e-guidebook: *Freedom from Clutter - Amy Anderson's Guide to Living your Life with Space to Spare*. It is, of course, available for digital download through my website.

First of all, it's important that you get rid of stuff every single day. Set aside small chunks of time specifically for de-cluttering. Fifteen to forty-five minutes a day probably works best. Any longer and you may become frustrated.

Choose a drawer, shelf or cluttered area and then just plunge in.

Take everything out one item at a time. And for every single thing ask yourself: do I need this? When was the last time I used it? Is this the right place for this particular item?

Then clean the space that you've emptied.

Now you're ready to put back only the articles that fit all three criteria: you need them, you use them and they belong in that specific spot.

Next decide what to do with the leftovers. Sort them into four piles: for storing in another location, for recycling, for re-purposing and for giving away.

Be ruthless about the things that you are holding on to or that you are planning on gifting.

Keep in mind not only your allotment capacity, but most importantly *The Naked Law* along with the other rules and regulations, especially *The No Gifting of Tangibles Law, The Grand Inventory*, *The Regulations for the Wise Use of Space,* and *The Rules for Downsizing*.

If you are torn in the difficult decision-making process, I advise you to err on the side of eliminating stuff.

If that makes you as anxious as it does most of us, then you might prefer creating a temporary "maybe box" in which you store stuff for one month.

That way, if you haven't used the items during that one month period of time, you will realize how useless they are to you and be more comfortable recycling or donating them.

I hope these hints help you.

Thank you for listening to me this evening. And now if there are any questions, I will be happy to answer them.

Sheri Does the Inventory Her Way!

Another immensely practical piece of metal that I own sits on my desk where it has served mainly as a paperweight. It has also come in handy as a hammer to pound that irritating little nail back into the floorboard, so that my sock won't get snagged, or worse, tear my barefoot skin.

This one pound lead weight is about the same vintage as the aluminum pot that I described earlier. It used to have a shiny silver coating, but that has mostly worn off. If you look closely though, you can still make out the one pound mark incised on its top.

Such archaic measurement devices were commonly used on mechanical scales to ensure the accuracy of what was weighed. In this case, one pound boxes of candied orange and lemon peel, maraschino cherries, dried fruit and ginger that were, and still are, I suppose, essential ingredients in Christmas and wedding cakes.

I know this with some certainty as I used this very tool for that purpose over the course of a summer when I worked in a canning factory in order to earn money for my university tuition fees. And at the end of my employment, I took the weight home as the one solid reminder of my first job.

Yes, I admit that I stole it. And in retrospect, my only excuse is rather feeble - the capriciousness of youth.

The city where I lived lay in the middle of the fertile fruit and vegetable producing area known then as the Niagara escarpment. When I was growing up, factories dedicated to canning, processing and otherwise preserving the bounty of the surrounding farms were everywhere.

The particular plant where I toiled was just a short walk from my home and although the work was hard, the pay was good for students. And I admit that joining the workforce that summer was an eye-opening experience.

Let me tell you first about punching in and punching out - a semi-automated method for keeping track of the time that you worked.

Each day when you arrived at the plant, you picked up a card with your name and employee number typed on it and inserted it into a box on the wall. A mechanism in the box imprinted the time on the card. When your shift was over, you popped the card back into the slot and the time that you finished work was punched on it.

You would then leave the card in a cubbyhole for the supervisor to collect. Your pay was based on your arrival and departure times as recorded on these cards.

Occasionally, employees knowing they were going to be late for work would ask co-workers to punch them in, thereby getting paid for time when they weren't on the job. Although most of us students were too scared to try the same trick, we quickly learned how easy it was to bilk the firm.

I'm not sure when this time-keeping system was replaced, if ever, as by the latter part of the 20th century most small food processing companies were no longer profitable and had shut down.

I don't think their closing was caused by pilfering of time, or of weights, but more likely because suburban sprawl had replaced fertile farm land with housing developments, mega shopping malls and super highways.

In addition to the arcane procedure for keeping track of employment hours, that summer job taught me that labouring in a factory was much like school - regimented and full of boring, repetitive tasks. But unlike school, the work had an actual result - a pay cheque every two weeks.

131

The full-time workers at the canning factory encouraged us students to do well at university, so that we would not have to end up like them, slaving in factories.

Unluckily for many of us, graduation led to office jobs that were no less constricted and also full of uninspiring, monotonous tasks. And the ambiguous results of our labour often seemed less fulfilling than the tangible goods produced at the plant.

Thus, my one pound tarnished weight is for me a potent symbol of that optimistic summer long ago when I first joined the workforce and when farming and processing food locally were sustainable industries. As such, it definitely belongs on my decidedly personal inventory of treasures.

Qs & As from the Clutter-Buster's Blog

Dear Clutter-Buster:

I just learned that my father-in-law has a secret collection of vintage 78s and LPs. What do I do? - *concerned*

Dear Concerned:

Before I answer your question, I want to let readers know what 78s and LPs are.

Now obsolete, phonographic records (flat discs with grooves in them) were analog sound storage media used for music reproduction until late in the 20th century.

78s refers to one of the common rotational speeds at which they were played. LP is a short form for long-playing and indicates their time capacity. Records required large electrical machines to operate.

Realizing that your father-in-law is a criminal can be devastating. Have you spoken to your husband about this shocking revelation?

Don't proceed with any action until you discuss his dad's crime with him. I think it's important that you both agree on how to approach his father and that you maintain a united stance when questioning him.

I would suggest that your husband first ask his dad to voluntarily inform the proper authorities about his stash.

You can provide your father-in-law with the contact information and any research that you have about the restitution that he will have to make for his offence.

If he refuses to turn himself in, then I'm afraid you have no recourse, but to inform the appropriate agency yourself. Let your father-in-law know that this is your intention and that if you do so, his punishment will be more severe. This knowledge might make him reconsider.

Museum of the Obsolete - Department Stores

Starting in the mid-19th century in major cities, retailers built large shopping emporiums that sold an eclectic variety of general merchandise under one roof. They were called department stores because they arranged their diverse goods into separate areas known as departments.

Most included departments for such goods as women's fashions, cosmetics, jewellery, men's apparel, children's clothes, shoes, fabrics, housewares, furniture, electrical appliances, books, toys, gourmet foods and sporting goods.

They also offered services including beauty salons, photo studios and restaurants to fully support the ever expanding culture of consumerism.

By the mid-20th century, these all-in-one marketplaces were thriving enterprises. And when the burgeoning middle class migrated to the suburbs after World War II, department stores sprouted auxiliary branches in shopping malls there.

Their growth halted during *The Decline* with the rise of specialized brick and mortar stores that ironically sold only one category of products.

In the end, the proliferation of online retailers, where you could get every type of merchandise imaginable, resulted in the extinction of the department store.

A Chorus of Voices
Party Ideas from Gail's Fun Galore Website

Hey followers, if you're looking for environmentally friendly ways to entertain your kids, you might want to check out gailsfungalore.uew. Here's a recent posting:

Got a party coming up? Try these hands-on non-competitive activities for children aged four to six. As well as having fun, your kids will learn valuable living tasks.

Rest assured that all the games have been pre-tested and approved by the Department of Recreation, Fitness and Sustainability. And they're definitely fun galore, or my name wouldn't be Gail.

Let's Pretend

Imagine that you are washed up on a desert island with one knapsack. What nine items would you want in it? Can you cut that list to five? How about two? If you were limited to just one thing, what would you keep?

Make up a story about it.

Instructions to party co-ordinator: this game works best

if you arrange the kids in a circle and give each a turn to talk about their nine items, then five, and then two, before telling their stories about that single most essential one.

The Magic Nine Circle Game

Go to the centre where the 3Ds are heaped. See how fast you can take a replica and put it in the correct receptacle. Remember that it's more important to put the thing in the right Magic Nine container than to do it quickly.

Instructions to party co-ordinator: affix a pictogram of each M9 resource - electronics, organics, paper, metal, glass, plastics, wood, appliances, and brokens - on to separate containers. And then arrange them in a circle.

Make 3Ds of a wide variety of valuable resources and place them in a pile in the middle.

Write a Poem

Choose nine pieces from the deck of cards in front of you. Flip them over to discover what nine words you have. Take your time and see if you can make a short poem that creates a picture or tells a story. You must use all of the nine words that you picked in your poem.

Once you are happy with your poem, copy it onto your tab. As soon as everyone is finished, take turns reading the poems aloud.

Instructions to party co-ordinator: create cards with the following words on them: squirrel, clutter, disarray, mess, litter, disorder, untidy, neat, tidy, muddle, strew, fill, cover, mess-up, fix, jumble, collector, saver, accumulator, magpie, renovate, organize, miser, stasher, repair, mend, put right, patch-up, arrange, sort, free, space, break.

Be sure to make enough, so each child can choose nine

pieces. It's OK to have multiple copies of the same word.

Make a Memory Box

Pretend that you are old and going to live in a care home. You will have a small cabinet with three shelves for storing your most precious things. This memory box is tiny, so you can only keep nine small trinkets in it.

Think about all your stuff. What nine items would you choose to display in your box? Which one is your favourite?

Instructions to party co-ordinator: if you can find an old-fashioned chalk board or an easel with paper, you might want to list their favourites there. Be sure to explain what these obsolete media are.

Otherwise, use your networked tabs to list these items.

The Seven Crimes of Consumerism

Not wanting to end my presentation on the gloomy note of automobiles and road rage, I will instead tell you briefly what the United Entities of the World is doing to ensure that the seven crimes of consumerism are held in check and that criminals are apprehended, fairly judged in a court of law, and appropriately disciplined.

Above all, we have *The Naked Law - Naked you came into this world, naked you must leave it.*

Upstanding citizens everywhere will adhere to this law and avoid committing any of the dastardly offences - Envy, Pride, Lust, Sloth, Greed, Gluttony and Wrath - that I have enumerated for you here today.

And as Global Government Advisors, you are more than familiar with *The Act Allowing Surveillance of Individuals and Corporations to Prevent Crimes against Humanity.*

This essential directive not only supports *The Naked Law,* but also all the 1,666 laws, acts and decrees enacted by the United Entities of the World after *The Great Resolve*.

You will also be aware of *The Global Criminal Code* and it is from that policy that I want to highlight for you a few of the laws specifically dealing with the seven crimes of consumerism. They are:

The Overconsumption Act
The Controlled Sale of Goods and Property Law
The Keeping the Resolve Decree
The Prohibited Goods Act
The Limitation of Growth Bill
The Downsizing Law, and
The Tackling Crimes of Overconsumption Regulation.

That concludes my address to you this evening and I will accept your questions now.

Sheri Does the Inventory Her Way!

Another of my most prized possessions, an actual paper book, is also quite practical. Its cover and front pages long gone, I can't tell you its name or who published it or when. Yet I know that it's at least as old as I am, and when I look at it, I tear up. It's so associated with my mother and with me as a young girl.

We always called it the cookie cook book, and now as I look through its torn and tattered pages held together with brittle yellow tape, I remember my mother and the many afternoons after school that we spent together working our way through these recipes.

At some point, we had decided to make every cookie in the book. And eventually, we did. Needless to say, we made our favourites more than once.

And as we completed and taste-tested each delight, we annotated the recipes for future reference with check marks, stars, and comments like "double the recipe," "less sugar," and "the best."

In spite of these notations, I can easily figure out which we most preferred - old-fashioned oatmeal cookies, charmin' cherry bars, jumble brownies - just by looking at the stain-encrusted pages.

The spotless recipes for such treats as French lace cookies or *pfeffernusse* clearly indicate those found wanting and not worth the effort.

Now I realize that the cookie cook book was a veritable baking compendium with simple, easy-to-follow instructions showing how to make perfect cookies of every kind: drop, moulded, bar, rolled, refrigerator and pressed, as well as cupcakes, pastry shells, éclairs, meringues and doughnuts.

The baking terms - sift together, cream, fold in, blend well, add gradually, beat - common then, seem like a foreign language nowadays.

As do some of the basic ingredients - shortening, cream of tartar, vanilla and almond extract, corn syrup, candied peel, rosewater and molasses.

All were ordinary staples of my mother's kitchen that I would have a hard time finding were I to bake any of these goodies today.

But really, who bakes anymore?

The time and the energy costs involved are considerable when compared with buying ready-made desserts. And yet the photos accompanying each recipe still tantalize.

So Steve, I will now pause in my story-telling inventory, make a list of exotic ingredients, and go shopping.

Museum of the Obsolete - Encyclopedias

Way before computers and online search engines, people accessed information in public libraries. These buildings contained a vast array of printed reference books including encyclopedias filled with alphabetically arranged, brief and pithy articles on thousands of subjects.

By far the most popular of these so called "books of knowledge" was the multi-volume *Encyclopedia Britannica*. Many middle-class families purchased individual sets for their personal use at home.

When it ceased publication in 2012, the *Encyclopedia Britannica* consisted of dozens of volumes weighing over one hundred pounds and costing more than one thousand dollars. The book format, the high price and the fact that it needed updating as soon as it was published contributed to its demise.

By that time too, the explosive rate of information growth precluded any possibility of publishing a comprehensive compendium of extant information in printed format.

And in fact, the prevalence of free online search engines effectively brought about the termination, not only of printed encyclopedias and all other reference books, but also of physical, bricks and mortar libraries.

Qs & As from the Clutter-Buster's Blog

Dear Clutter-Buster:

My guy has two turtles and I have a cat. When we get married, we are only allowed two pets under *The Animal Control Bylaw*.

I suggested keeping one turtle and my cat. He balks at breaking up his twosome. I think this might be the marriage-buster. Any advice? - *cat-lover*

Dear Cat-Lover:

It's difficult to split a pair and it's tough to give up your pet. This is the first of many dilemmas that you will face as a married couple, so you are right to be troubled about his adamant stance.

Together, you will have to come to a mutually agreeable resolution to this problem. And whatever the decision, the two of you will need to lovingly accept it.

You do not want to deal with recriminations whenever you have a disagreement in the future.

I suggest that you sit down with your husband-to-be and discuss the issue calmly. It will be challenging and both of you must resist the urge to be angry and argumentative.

It may help to remind yourself that you are having a conversation with the person you love and with whom you want to spend the rest of your life. Good luck.

A Chorus of Voices - The Knitter Comes Undone

It seemed so useless, didn't it? All that time, all that effort. Oh well, I guess the joy and the benefits were in the doing, not in the finishing of the task. And for this end-of-life project, there was no completion possible, was there?

I would just continue knitting until the end. His end, I mean. And with his final breath, I would begin the frogging. I would start unravelling all that I had done during the months that I sat at his bedside.

Click-clack, my needles went throughout the first days

and nights of hopefulness, then during the long period of giving up any expectations, and finally, when I was just hanging on. Waiting.

Click-clack. I found a measure of calmness clutching those batons although I could orchestrate nothing.

Click-clack. Knit one, purl two, over and over again in an endless refrain that I didn't want to silence.

Click-clack and I didn't have to look at what I was doing. I could watch him, see him breathe.

Observe them too, coming and going, looking after him. Take it all in like Madame Defarge.

So I knitted, but now comes the undoing. And it seems as if my mind is coming apart, too. With every rip out, I moan. With every row opened, I weep.

Knitting is making something. Creating even if there is no purpose to it.

Frogging is a big step backwards. Soul destroying.

But alas, I think that it's symptomatic of everything that's wrong with society today.

Damn that *Anti-Craft Law*. You can't buy supplies to make things. You have to deplete what you already have and when that's all used up, you can only make something fresh if you're willing to work over the old.

Or the item that you create has to be ephemeral like chalk painting or sand sculptures.

Knit bombing is completely outlawed although Stitch 'n' Bitch groups are still allowed as long as members unravel anything produced during a session.

All very Zen, but, blast it all, I liked being able to make something and give it to someone.

Of course people nowadays don't accept gifts anyway. If you were foolish enough to offer them something, they act as if you were trying to get them to break the law.

Which I suppose you are. *The No Gifting of Tangibles Law* was one of the earliest edicts. In one swoop, it did away with all rite of passage and Christmas presents.

But I must say that consumerism did get way out of hand during *The Decline*.

It seemed then as if everyone completely lost their sense of restraint and their ability to celebrate in meaningful ways. As if life was only about reckless buying, impressing others, fulfilling every whim, and satisfying every urge.

Yet hand-crafted gifts always seemed better somehow than manufactured stuff. At least by us makers, they did. Although I expect that they weren't really. For they were items that someone still had to deal with, look after, and dispose of eventually.

I, a harmless crafter, was right up there with all the other nasty producers of things. Oh, the shame of it all.

The sheer embarrassment of making useless objects and contributing to the glut.

Yes, I suppose that in most instances, you shouldn't do it at all. No knitting, no sewing, no needlepoint.

However to sit with Fred, I needed something tactile to distract my mind and to soothe my soul.

Knitting served that purpose for me. And now I must pay for my indulgence. So I will unravel all my work and try hard not to lose my mind at the same time.

There's no peace in frogging although, I guess, in a way I'm reaping what I sewed. LOL.

And what will I do with the pile of wool once undone? What can I do with it?

Solving that is a whole new project. Let me figure out how to get rid of a heap of yarn.

I could pass it on to another knitter - someone who has not exhausted her lifetime fibre quota. Or I could offer it secretly to a rebel crafter.

How about taking it with me on a walk and disposing of it surreptitiously?

Except, what if I was caught? It would be so shameful. I can't imagine what Mikey and Erin would think about their grandma then.

I could knit bomb and have a blast doing it, at least until I was arrested. But then, what kind of example would I be to the kids?

Easiest way might be to cut up the wool into little pieces and throw it bit by bit down the toilet or bury it in the yard.

Or why not just hide it in the house?

But that would leave the problem for the next generation. My heirs. That's a funny word to use nowadays when no one is allowed to inherit anything. And that would surely be an unkind burden to lay upon them anyway.

I think it's best if I leave the yarn and the knitting needles at the hospice for others to use when they are there waiting. That way the yarn could be worked over and over again.

I will see if that is allowed. What a blessing to bestow on that little mound of fibre. Sounds a bit blasphemous though, so I mustn't phrase it that way when I ask.

Sheri Does the Inventory Her Way!

And now Steve, I want to share with your followers, the story of a piece of furniture that combines the practicality of my much-used metal pot with the wondrous beauty of my Moroccan rocks. It also incorporates the metamorphic quality inherent in the Mdina glass that I described earlier.

We acquired an onyx-topped, oval-shaped coffee table in the early years of our marriage. And it has been front and centre in every living room in all the places that we've since called home.

The hefty three by four foot, highly polished slab of green crystalline rock rests solidly on a Bauhaus-style pedestal of russet mahogany.

Over the years, it has served multiple purposes.

It was, first and foremost, an elegant coffee table covered with delectable canapés and drinks during many pleasant and stimulating soirées with friends.

More often than not though, the table was piled high with the books, newspapers and magazines that were essential to our happiness and well-being.

Sometimes it was used as a foot-rest, and at other times, it was the perfect place for sorting and collating documents or arranging photographs into an album.

On more than one occasion, it morphed into an exciting games table. The mahogany that framed the smooth onyx proved to be an ideal race car track and marbles rolled easily around its rim.

The table's large expanse made it especially appropriate for spreading out jigsaw puzzles and playing leisurely card games like *Concentration*.

Does anyone else besides me remember those slow and gentle pre-computer pastimes?

I certainly recall many an evening spent playing *Solitaire* on that table while waiting for Karen's return from a date.

Less traditionally, it functioned as an impromptu diaper change table - the only clean, solid and uncluttered surface available at times.

To be sure, I liked the table most when it was bare, so

that I could clearly appreciate the mottled patterns that made up its amazing surface. Mineral impurities deposited in the rock eons ago created myriad earth-coloured veins.

I can't tell you how many pleasant hours I spent utterly mesmerized by the visions I conjured in its serpentine swirls. The configurations seemed to change, depending on which side of the table I was sitting on, or where the sunlight dappled it.

And on more occasions than I like to recollect, it served as my de-facto psychiatrist-in-residence.

Emotionally ravaged by some upset, or wobbly and overwhelmed by life, I would lose myself in the depths of the tabletop's variegated landscape and after a while find my balance again.

Just as the accretions in the onyx added to its fascination, so too did a thread-like fissure meandering from one side of its surface to the other.

That hairline fracture had been essential to our possessing this wonderful table in the first place.

No, not because we liked the crack. But because the barely visible fault in the stone made the piece damaged goods, so that we got to purchase it at a fraction of its worth.

A *wabi-sabi* break indeed!

Since then the flaw has been joined by many other nicks and abrasions. Some memorable like the diamond-shaped gouge made by a toy car hurled on to it during a three-year-old's temper tantrum; others are lost to time.

Yes, this table was destined to be ours.

And now infused with our personal family history, it has turned into an enduring palimpsest of our lives - much, much more than just a piece of furniture on an inventory list.

Random Notes on *The Decline*
Revitalizing the Bees

Hello blog followers. Today's offbeat history lesson comes from Miranda Darwell.

Bees have been pollinating plants for fifty million years. Without these industrious insects, one third of the world's food crops, including apples, almonds, watermelons and beans, could not reproduce.

These tiny creatures are so important that Albert Einstein warned, "If the bee disappeared off the surface of the globe, then man would have only four years of life left. No more bees, no more pollination, no more plants, no more animals, no more man."

During *The Decline*, scientists reported that bees were vanishing and their colonies collapsing at an unprecedented rate. They blamed the devastating degree of insect deaths on habitat destruction and identified the likely source as the agricultural conglomerates' ever-increasing specialization in monoculture crop production and their extensive over-use of insecticides to improve yields and boost profits.

Echoing Einstein, experts around the world advised that this pandemic would inflict tragic consequences not only on plant life, but also on the very survival of humankind.

As time went on, consumers did in fact notice that fewer varieties of fruit and vegetables were available in grocery stores. Yet little was done to curb the dwindling of bee populations before *The Final Catastrophe*.

During *The Great Resolve*, the United Entities of the World began the arduous and critical process of revitalizing the earth's agricultural land masses. One of their first deeds was to completely ban the production of neonicotinoids and other lethal insecticides.

By taking this imperative action, the UEW substantially increased the likelihood that bees would once again flourish and that Mother Earth would ultimately recover from the desecration caused by greed and indifference.

Qs & As from the Clutter-Buster's Blog

Dear Clutter-Buster:

My roommate was directed to dispose of a collection of old family photographs after being turned down twice for an exemption. I thought that she had gotten rid of them although she never talked about it.

Last week, I noticed that her desk drawer was sporting a new lock and I now suspect that she has hidden the illegal photos there. Should I confront her? - *curious*

Dear Curious:

You have a right to be concerned and a conversation with her is in order. But be prepared to find another roommate as such seemingly innocent discussions often lead to big, ugly brouhahas.

At the very least, she may accuse you of snooping. And what were you doing examining her desk, anyway?

Museum of the Obsolete - Movie Theatres

Movie theatres or cinemas were commercial venues located in buildings and shopping malls where people would pay to watch movies. They ranged from intimate spots seating under a hundred people to multiplexes with a capacity for thousands.

Throughout the 20th century, going to a movie was a common social outing. People bought tickets for a film, lined up and then found seats in the theatre. At scheduled times, a movie was projected onto a large screen at the front of a darkened auditorium. Snacks such as popcorn, candy and soft drinks were offered for sale.

During *The Decline*, attendance at movie theatres rapidly waned. People preferred to be entertained in the privacy and comfort of their own homes. Thus, watching films on cable television or streaming them to personal devices prevailed. These methods also allowed for an infinite variety of films to be screened according to an individual's own schedule.

By the time of *The Final Catastrophe*, movie theatres had ceased operation and their buildings were abandoned.

A Chorus of Voices
Melvin Cries Over Broken Eggs

Hey Steve, I know this is a bit of a downer, but I just need to unload. And *In the Middle of Things* seems like as good a place as any to let go.

I've been getting really depressed with some of my latest assignments. Yesterday, for example, I had to photograph a collection of rare birds' eggs. Knowing that they were all going to be mulched as soon as I scanned them into the archive made me feel like throwing up. I wanted to stop, to delay, to procrastinate, big time!

I couldn't help but think of the explorers over a century

ago who had travelled the world, risking their lives to gather and bring these precious eggs back, so that thousands of people could see these priceless natural wonders. And here I am destroying them.

Yeah, I realize that those discoverers were thieves and I appreciate that it's only a job and that if I didn't do it, they would hire someone else.

Still, day-in, day-out, this kind of mass obliteration of extraordinary things makes me want to flat out quit.

I feel like just taking off and sitting on a bench in a park somewhere and feeding the pigeons. At least then I would be doing something worthwhile.

I know that the eggs themselves are useless. I recognize too that it's better for people to just view the images.

And I understand that with 3D they can even feel them, but it just seems so dreadfully wrong.

Damn all those collectors. Now we have to deal with the fallout from their hoarding compulsions, and it totally sucks to be the one doing it.

Sheri Does the Inventory Her Way!

The Essential Goods Inventory form has no category that does justice to the final item that I will use to argue my case for changing it. And just like the onyx-topped coffee table, chance also played a part in how I acquired *Yesterday's Perfume*, the first piece of art I ever bought.

Much more than a lovely wall decoration, this quirky assemblage uncannily reflected so many of my passions that it quickly became an essential part of my very being. And I can no more imagine living without it than doing without food, water, or any of my most cherished belongings.

I was unusually early for a dinner engagement and so decided on the spur of the moment to drop into an art gallery next to the restaurant. This was at a time when I was young and quite self-conscious and when galleries were pretentious places. So it was rather brave of me to pull open the gallery's heavy wooden door and enter at all.

Once inside, I felt a bit awkward because I knew nothing about contemporary art and had no intentions other than passing the time. Therefore, I was relieved that the person behind the desk at the back of the gallery was on the phone and barely acknowledged my presence.

It was summer and what I now know to be the off-season when galleries frequently fill their walls with work by lesser known artists. So I meandered through a rather hodgepodge exhibition of abstract art called *Patchwork*.

I paused in front of each artwork for a moment or two until I reached a fairly large creation covered with odds and ends of all manner of stuff - miniature photographs, shiny buttons, glittery jewellery, tiny perfume bottles, nuggets of broken china, textured lace and velvet pieces.

All these delightful bits and bobs were meticulously arranged in a wooden typesetter's tray, transforming it into a compelling, and to my mind, quite magical reliquary.

I was enchanted. This singular artwork evoked in me an ethereal mood of wistful melancholy - a kind of nostalgic yearning that I had felt before, but never seen expressed in such a powerfully bittersweet way.

When I checked the label, I was stunned to learn that *Yesterday's Perfume* had been created by none other than my own amazing sister, Lena Lorca.

Somehow she had captured my soul - or maybe hers - in

this one incredible piece of art.

Unable to fully absorb this revelation before hurrying off, I noted the price of this shamanistic piece which was more than I could afford on my meagre copywriter's salary.

At dinner though and in the days following, all I could think about was Lena's piece. I rationalized how I could save money by not eating out and foregoing taxis, so that I would be able to purchase it.

Or perhaps, I could suck up to my big sister in the hopes that she would come forward with a family price.

Was this the beginning of my lifelong collector-mania?

A foretaste of the endless bargains and trade-offs that I would continue to make with myself whenever I wanted to buy something.

Whatever. The very thought of possessing *Yesterday's Perfume* consumed me like some new love.

A few days later, having resolved not to ask Lena for a bargain, I found myself back in the gallery. And ignoring all the other art, I zeroed in on my obsession and when the exhibition closed a few weeks later, I eagerly took it home.

It's hard to believe now that getting it was happenstance. A twist of fate that in retrospect proved to be not just life-enhancing, but truly transforming.

For *Yesterday's Perfume* was my introduction not only to Lena's secretive life work, but also to an entire world of creative people involved not in pursuing traditional, money-oriented success, but rather in chasing their dreams.

Today, this remarkable creation hangs over my beloved washstand and continues to provide never-ending sustenance for my soul, along with its surprisingly profound personal connection. And like all my worldly goods, I have never regretted acquiring it.

Intermezzo

Rest not! Life is sweeping by;
go dare before you die.
Something mighty and sublime,
leave behind to conquer time.
- *Johann Wolfgang von Goethe*

Ode IV

… Don't ask (it's forbidden to know) what final fate the gods have given to me and you … How much better it is to accept whatever shall be, whether Jupiter has given many more winters or whether this is the last one ... Be wise, strain the wine, and trim distant hope within short limits. While we're talking, grudging time will already have fled: seize the day, trusting as little as possible in tomorrow. - *Horace*

The Story of Scheherazade in *The Thousand and One Nights*

Every day the king would marry a new virgin and every day he would send yesterday's wife to be beheaded. This was done in anger, having found out that his first wife was unfaithful to him. He had killed one thousand such women by the time he was introduced to Scheherazade.

In Sir Richard Burton's translation of *The Thousand and One Nights*, Scheherazade was described in this way:

"[Scheherazade] had perused the books, annals and legends of preceding Kings, and the stories, examples and instances of bygone men and things; indeed it was said that she had collected a thousand books of histories relating to antique races and departed rulers.

She had perused the works of the poets and knew them by heart; she had studied philosophy and the sciences, arts and accomplishments; and she was pleasant and polite, wise and witty, well read and well bred.

Against her father's wishes, Scheherazade volunteered to spend one night with the King. Once in the King's chambers, Scheherazade asked if she might bid one last farewell to her beloved sister, Dinazade, who had secretly been prepared to ask Scheherazade to tell a story during the long night. The King lay awake and listened with awe as Scheherazade told her first story. The night passed by, and Scheherazade stopped in the middle of the story.

The King asked her to finish but Scheherazade said there was not time as dawn was breaking. So the King spared her life for one day to finish the story the next night.

So the next night, Scheherazade finished the story and then began a second, even more exciting tale which she again stopped halfway through, at dawn. So the King again spared her life for one day to finish the second story.

And so the King kept Scheherazade alive day by day as he eagerly anticipated the finishing of last night's story. At the end of one thousand and one nights, and one thousand stories, Scheherazade told the King that she had no more tales to tell him.

During these one thousand and one nights, the King had fallen in love with Scheherazade and had three sons with her.

So having been made a wiser and kinder man by Scheherazade and her tales, he spared her life and made her his Queen."

Part II

The Artist Contemplates Her Demise

Yeah, I just got the news. It ain't good. Six months at the most. Crap, crap, crap. Why me? But then again, why not, eh? The worst of it is - well, maybe not the worst - still, what a fuck-up to think that I have to spend my remaining time going through all my stuff and getting rid of it.

Not the regular things - I was never much of a collector, so that won't take too long. But my artwork.

All the pieces that I produced before the law, some of which I have exemptions for. And all that I made after; most of which I didn't, according to the decree, "cover over if in excess of twelve each year."

No BS, I've got lots to dump. But first, I have to gather them. Yep, they're stored in all sorts of places - among friends, with relatives, in hideaways, in closets and covert storage lockers - you name it.

Dammit all, this is major and really not what I want to think about right now.

No, I would like to spend the last six months, or however many days I'm blessed with, enjoying life on this still, much beloved planet and, I hate to say it, creating one last final piece of art.

A painting that says me, that won't be destroyed, that will be kept, that will last forever. A work of art that will earn itself an exemption *extraordinaire*.

Yet how can I focus when I've got all these other things to do? It's not just finding, listing and disposing of my art. No, it's all the forms and duties that must be completed now that I know my end is near.

Just locating all my art will take some doing. I'll need to go through my journals, put together a list, and see if I can unearth every one of my pieces and every place where I've squirreled my work away.

Squirreled, ha, ha.

But I'm past the season of mellow fruitfulness. Now the winter of my discontent is upon me and I need to find the nuts that I've hidden, stored for just such a dismal season.

Yes, yes, everybody's got to go some time, except I'm not the least bit ready. I can be thankful though that I didn't get hit by a moto and just expired then and there, or had a heart conk out, or any number of other sudden exits.

Although then I wouldn't have had to worry about all the laws that I broke with my art.

Still, it wouldn't have been fair to my friends and my kin who helped me stash the stuff. It would be leaving a lot of extra tasks for them.

Most awful, an abrupt departure wouldn't have let me make more art. It wouldn't have let me create my definitive piece - the finest accomplishment of my life's work.

My *pièce de résistance*.

Oh my, how I've suddenly segued into French as if that's a better, more refined way of dealing with this mess, the chaos of my life. But I must think about that.

Let me just Amazoogle a bit: "*Pièce de résistance* refers to the best part of something, a showpiece or highlight. It is the portion of a creation that defies common conventions and is the most outstanding or defining of the collection.

"The term is also used for the last piece to complete the build as when someone finishes something and says: 'and now, the *pièce de résistance*' ...."

The last piece to complete the build.

I like that. That sense that all my paintings have been building towards a pinnacle and that my life's output won't be complete without this ultimate showpiece. The painting that will define my life's work. The capstone!

My *pièce de résistance* will be a work so spectacular that no one will be able to ignore it.

Yes, in my final blow-out, I will fight against my own inhibitions and defy the restrictions of the law.

This last creation will totally transcend the deficiencies of all my previous works.

Take it easy, Lena. Slow down. Be calm. Deep breathes now. Inhale ... one, two, three. Exhale. Let it all out. A little meditation to soothe the agitation ... ah, that's better.

But do I want to waste my so very valuable remaining time turning off and blissing out?

Time enough later for such foolishness when that's all that's left to me. Plenty of time for that in the great beyond. The timeless void.

Dancing around the void. That's what we do, isn't it?

I think I have a painting somewhere by that same name. Fuck, I remember that I did a whole show with that title.

The painting came about after my awful accident. It was certainly therapeutic.

I have it somewhere. It didn't sell, like a lot of my works. Too dark, too filled with intense, ugly, frightening emotions. Hell, it even scared me!

A hot bath? No, no, no! I think it's more appropriate that I take out of my support arsenal, my weapons of choice - a vintage bottle of red, real cancer-inducing sticks, a classic fountain pen, and a pad of parchment paper.

Aha, what joy! What freaking, so good indulgence. So wicked, so sinful. Thank you, Jimmy!

Yes, I deserve to sit in my inglenook, near the window that looks outside to the garden patch and unhurriedly make my list.

No dammit, not my last will and testament. I still have time for that. Rather a record of my art. A fucking inventory, but for my eyes only.

Damn those government auditors, officious bureaucraps. I want to create a calligraphic catalogue of my life's *oeuvre*.

Again with the French!

Funny, but things do sound better in that language.

Why? I don't know. I guess that's the reason a trip to old Montreal always brought out the aesthete in me.

Anyhow I need to make this *memento mori* on a concrete, not virtual, medium - sheets of old-fashioned writing paper inscribed with ink, a fluid that flows like the blood when you slit your wrists.

And of course, the wine that I will sip as I go through this gruelling process will be a fine French *Bordeaux*.

Do I have any tucked away?

Ha, unlikely. No *cache du vin* for me. And since wine cellars were one of the storage things banned at the time of *The Great Resolve*, it would need to be illicit anyway, and I've got enough unlawful things going on in my life.

Ciggies. Well, why not unfiltered *Gitanes*?

I think I can risk getting hooked now since I've already drawn a different death card.

Then again, do real cigarettes still exist? It's been years since I've seen anyone smoking. Are they even legal?

Who grows tobacco anymore? Are people in China or India manufacturing them? Can you still smoke there?

No way do I want e-ciggies, those grown-up pacifiers. No pizzazz there. I'll have to check online for real cancer sticks. I wonder if there's a black market for them.

What the hell does black market mean? How did it get into my mind? Absorbed through the *Zeitgeist*?

Let me just look it up: "A black market or underground economy is the market in which goods or services are traded illegally. The key distinction of a black market trade is that the transaction itself is illegal. The goods or services may or may not be illegal to own, or to trade through other, legal channels."

Wow. I had an inkling, but really all the terms that I don't fully understand. I'll die not knowing what I don't know. There's so much out there, isn't there? And I've surely only scratched the surface.

Our lives are lived small - ha, another title of a forgotten painting that I did long ago. So friggin' small.

A record of my artwork. Find them. Where are they? Start with their titles.

Can I do that? Can I remember them all?

First, I'll have to check my website.

Did I do an archive in my ambitious, organizing days? If so, on what cloud did I store it?

What about submission files?

Ha! Rejection letters are more like it.

Journals? Sure, if I kept notes on my works.

Oh crap. I only wrote when things were going badly, when I wasn't creating at all.

It would have been so easy to methodically keep track of my artwork as I completed each piece. I've heard that some artists do that. But fuck, I was all over the place.

While I was painting, I was working like I was in heat. I certainly didn't fuss over chronicling anything.

And when I wasn't creating, I was depressed. I couldn't have listed my art if I wanted to. In that state, it was as if I had done nothing. Nothing worth anything, anyway.

Don't go there girl, don't go there now.

Later, once you've done your accounting, finished the review; then you can summarize, total up, analyse your life. Decide too, if it was worth it.

I know it's still morning; nonetheless, I'm going to have a glass of chilled *Chardonnay*, a slice of smoked salmon, cream cheese and capers on a crusty *baguette*.

Treat myself well from here on in. If I want something, I'll have it. No more hemming and hawing, weighing the consequences. Diets be damned. Cardio health? Forget it. I've got enough heart to get me through the next six months.

My time is now. Here and now for pleasure. My life is too short for anything else. Thank you, Martha!

So here I am - sitting in limbo with vague memories.

I have a few catalogues from exhibitions. I can start there although mostly I need to search out and gather my works. Then consider each of them with a critical eye.

I must take the time to gaze at them lovingly for they are truly my babies and will be orphaned soon enough.

Yes, they are the ones. They harbour in their paint all my passions. My loves, hates, anger, joys, lust. All the crazy obsessions and enthusiasms of my life.

Plus all the anxieties that it took to make them. And all the ruminations that creating them took me away from. All the traces of people, places and objects I've loved, and lost.

Oh my, I will need several bottles, won't I?

It's so upsetting looking back. Always was. That's why I avoided it. One glance at a painting could rip me apart with the sensations of when I made it. All flooding back, horrible!

Dammit, I don't want to make this my *annus horribilis*, although it will be, won't it?

Are there people I should tell? Share this ghastly news with? Does anybody care?

Well, yes, naturally, when they hear about it they will be sad, shocked even. Yet truly, everyone will go on with their own lives. They will keep going and it's only me who won't.

Perhaps letting them know will remind them of their ultimate fate, and maybe they will think twice about what they are now doing. Pay attention to the present. But I think at most that will only last for a few days, if that.

Cynical maybe. However I've heard enough devastating news over the years. Disturbing for sure. Shed a few tears, shared some drinks and commiserated, but then, with a sigh, moved on to my own problems *du jour*.

Zut alors! Impending death surely brings out the Gallic in me. I wouldn't have guessed that. Would have thought that I'd be more Swedish, more Bergmanesque in my final act.

But who knows; that might come. It ain't over yet. And perhaps, it's just revealing the morose French side of my nature, the other solitude of being a true Canadian.

What about setting down my thoughts? Writing a memoir or maybe even a blog?

My Final Days by Lena Lorca.

What a waste that would be, a grasping, freaking, awful way of striving for immortality.

Not for me.

I need to keep doing what I've always done, except with more verve and more zest than I've had in many years. Kick out the jams, go to the edge, just do it. Thank you, Nike!

Hey, no more need to wish I exercised more, was an athlete, ran a marathon, jogged my way to health and fitness.

Yes, I can create my piece. I can because my mind won't be fucking full of other things - all the shouldas, wouldas, couldas, and the if-onlys.

To be sure, I may not have left the land of if-onlys yet. I suppose that I'm there now, but the shouldas, wouldas, couldas, those can be ditched right away. Especially as far as physical fitness is concerned.

I'm not talking walking. Walking is life to me and I will continue to stride, to amble, to look, to see - that's me, that's my way, that won't change.

But damn all their wise words - you're tall, you should play basketball. Long legs, you'd make a good runner. You don't need booze, working out raises the endorphins. Join a gym, live forever, stay in the garden, never grow old.

Come on, get real. The big C or something else will get you in the end. It's only a matter of when.

Isn't that what we've grappled with all our lives?

How to make the best use of our limited time on earth. How to spend it. How to waste it.

Time is money! That's a joke, isn't it?

Wealth can't buy anyone more moments. Look at that early computer whiz Steve Jobs. All his riches. Fought 'til the bitter end, trying to postpone his fate.

Well, that's futile, isn't it? Death gets everyone.

Who's going to miss you when you're gone?

These lyrics have already become my earworm. But crap, I ain't got nobody really. Not a soul left. No one.

I don't feel down about it. It's just the way it is. How it worked out.

There were times when I had people who cared. Who liked me, loved me even, as I did them. Now they're either dead or far away like Dad and Sheri. Gone for good anyway.

The Artist Reviews Her Work

However these exhibition catalogues are here - permanent records of segments of my past, and just what I need at this particular moment.

I always felt I should review my artwork and enumerate it, too. But I just never got around to it. Too busy making more, I guess.

So terribly diligent that I never took the time to see where I was coming from. To examine the path I'd been following and perhaps get new directions for a fresh route. For sure, I was neglecting the pause that refreshes.

Goddess knows, my art could have used a boost. Even last week, a review of my past works might have got me out of my aimless hole. If only I had pushed myself to look back, to face the abyss through my work.

Who knows what jazzy inspirations might have come out of those blues? What juicy new creations?

Instead I was stuck in a rut. Coasting easy, but rudderless. Making the same old facile marks that always worked. Until they didn't.

Comfy, but not carefree. Haunted by the habitual angst that I should be stretching way beyond the *laissez-faire*.

Digging deep into the cracks. Because I know that's where the light gets in. I know because Leonard told me so.

Well, now I'm forced to take a breather. Time out from my toil to reflect on the veracity of my life. The fickle finger of fate has me in its grasp and that's no laughing matter.

So let me pour myself another glass of wine and peruse a few relics from the archives of my past.

Aha - the catalogue for *Life Matters* is a good place to start my review as I can't imagine that life could matter any more to me than it does right at this moment.

Also, my exhibition by that name was a pivotal milestone in my career. I remember that the works in that show had morphed into a rather unusual conceptual mode that I hadn't attempted until then.

Life Matters - Artist's Statement

"These minimalist pieces are structured around the mutability of life. They sketch out little spots of recognition along the journey of our lives from the tomb of the womb to the womb of the tomb.

"In addition to recording the mundane cycle of trifling defeats and squandered opportunities, the works explore the unframed, raw edges of existence where life turns on a dime. The times when events confound us or when tragedy strikes, and we fully realize the tenuousness of our lives.

"A recurring theme is the fragility of life and how we can best respond to that delicate framework with its sudden shifts in direction, tone and mood.

"And because we cannot know what is to come; we can merely dance the dance until the end of the song.

"Only life, death and regeneration are the eternal verities - the truth of the cosmos."

I can still drink to that creed. *In vino veritas*.

Anyhow, my life has definitely turned on a dime. Went to bed last night, dreamt my usual dreams, planned my typical day and then the fucking news that changed everything.

Or maybe, changed nothing.

Oh well. Here's another title in the series that's dead on - *Facing the Abyss*.

I may have thought that I confronted it before. Stared it down. Nevertheless, here it is back again. Big time. And I truly must come to grips with it now.

Black Bad for sure. Yet another painting that I made for a different dark time.

Without a doubt, I feel like I'm living my art. I created these pieces shortly after my accident. Having survived, I was buoyant with a mind-blowing sense of *joie de vivre* and a single-minded determination not simply to carry on, but to make my work trip the light fantastic.

Producing the art though was a slippery slide through more than one bed of nettles. And instead of the edenic series that I imagined, I ended up with soul-baring works full of regrets and desolation. Dark flowers from the garden of Gethsemane.

In *Summer of the Empty Pots*, my thoughts were focused on the many torpid and thorny periods when a profound weariness enshrouded me, body and soul.

During those heavy times, I couldn't summon up the energy or the inclination to even venture outside, never mind making it into the garden. So the planters stayed unfilled from spring to fall.

Then in the winter, I would sit by the window and think how satisfying those pots looked, packed to their brims with clean white snow. Like blank canvases.

Occasionally, I would imagine the pots overflowing with

colourful harbingers of spring - crocuses, tulips, daffodils and hyacinths. And afterwards I would make a list of bulbs and seeds to buy.

However when spring unexpectedly burst forth, I would crumple up my plans. Planting seemed like too much bother. And the flowers would only wither and die anyway.

I remember another work from that sequence that seemed to be just a straightforward exploration in minimalism. But now as I add it to my compendium, I feel that *Our Lives Are Lived Small* cries out for elucidation.

It's not that I mean that we are diminutive in the grand scheme of things, although we are. In this painting, I'm suggesting only that most of our lives are not celebrity big. We aren't fodder for the latest tweet.

Our existence passes by like "a shadow moving on" and few see the ever-changing and intricate interplay of light and dark that we radiate. In truth, hardly anyone even notices that we have come, danced, and left the party.

Yet we get so mired in the bits and blogs, tweets and chatter of the electronic airways, that we often lose our way. We forget that these stars form just an infinitesimal part of earth's six billion people.

Billions of bright lights flickering in the sky, but only a few bedazzlers are visible to the naked eye.

So in this work, I tried to cut through the din and show simply that each of our lives counts. That every single one of our lives is worth celebrating.

Life Mutates Without Warning. The penny drops. No explanation is required for that work.

Why did the pretty guitarist with the sweet smile go to sleep one night and not wake up in the morning? Why did the young mom out jogging get killed by a car as she crossed the street? Why did the old man, strolling in the sunshine, fall, break his hip and die? Why did the artist get cancer and have only six months to live?

Why indeed?

But why not, too? *C'est la vie*. Just accept.

Ten years separated my *Life Matters* exhibition from the *Dancing Around the Void* show; however, I see that in my art I was still trying to figure out the meaning of life and make sense of its intrinsic ambiguities.

Dancing Around the Void - Artist's Statement

"In these paintings, I am exploring those moments of luminosity and understanding that hover between being and non-being. How the chaos of life in its infinite complexity resolves itself in death and regeneration.

"For several years, I have been delving into the yin/yang of this life-dance-void experience. Existentially, we dance constantly around the void, trying to accumulate meaning. We may live in the here and now, but there is always a big emptiness that surrounds us.

"With these works, allusions to both personal traumas and global tragedies abound. And in the end, dancing in the face of the abyss is all that anyone can do. That is the reality that everyone must come to terms with."

Wow, that sounds pretty good, doesn't it? Amazing that I painted that series and wrote this long before *The Final Catastrophe*. I haven't re-read it for more than twenty years.

Nonetheless, if I knew all that then, why didn't I live the last two decades differently? There's the question.

Too much time hovering in the chaos, methinks. And really, very little brightness and even less clarity.

But then again, what was the alternative?

I remember well my crazy desperation when I painted

Phoenix Rising (After the Fall).

And I'm still moved when I see it every day, as it's one of the few of my works that I've hung in my home, rather appropriately, I think, over the fireplace.

In that painting, I was going deeply into the death and resurrection myth and the idea that we can recover after a catastrophic event. At the time, I believed fervently that we mortal beings are constantly falling, picking up the pieces, and then starting all over again.

And even though I continue to see optimism in that drive to survive, I'm afraid that outlook won't help me face this final chapter of my life.

I can't envision a way out of my predicament. No new beginnings for me.

Around the same time as *Phoenix Rising*, I created *Hidden in Plain Sight (Ariel)*, my homage to Plath.

Yes, I certainly could relate to another badly wounded sensitive who dodged her demons in such a tragic manner.

I think that it's fair to surmise that most of us who thrash about in our messy lives have sometimes craved burrowing in a closet or under the stairs and, dare I admit it, even pined for a total dissolve.

And more than a few of us have found it necessary from time to time to actually withdraw into lonely places, virtual spaces, and the solitude of our minds.

But fortunately, unlike dear Sylvia, most of us eventually emerge from our sanctuary a bit more bruised, but still able to keep on dancing.

Yes, we continue to whirl and spin in fast moving circles round the chaos - undoubtedly more like dervishes than ballerinas - until the inevitable standstill.

For absolutely no one escapes the final reality.

The Artist Dawdles

I suppose that looking through my exhibition catalogues has provided me with a starting point for my inventory. Now I'd best find somewhere special to log my works.

No, I'm not going to use the mandatory Inventory of Items for Disposal on Death form. Let the bureaucraps fill out docs. My time is limited.

I'll venture instead into my creative kitchen. The place that my sister Sheri loves so much when she visits.

It's the room where I hoard all my bits and pieces for making. Shards of old glass, cracked bowls, damaged dolls, fragments of broken china, feathers, buttons, bones, corks, flotsam and jetsam, baubles and beads.

And on shelves I've stored a collector's delight of vintage magazines, swatches of fabric and leather, period postcards and old books.

Good grief, with all this incredible stuff, it's a wonder that I haven't created something original and magnificent like Frankenstein did.

Anyhow, somewhere in this delightful mess of promise, I must have a journal full of empty pages waiting to be filled. The perfect place to record the creations of a lifetime.

Unlike some artists in the past, I don't have the funds to build a memorial gallery where my works could be displayed in perpetuity.

What blatant narcissism that would be in any case. And I can see why after *The Great Resolve*, the UEW banned the erection of any more structures to ego and systematically disassembled existing collections, re-purposing the buildings that housed them for more practical uses.

Likewise, I fully understand their reasons for limiting the

amount of art that one could not only keep, but also make. If I had only complied with their restrictions, I would surely be having an easier time of it now.

Oh goody, I've found a shelf laden with blank journals, writing pads and sketch books. Some with leather-bound, embossed covers that I long ago stockpiled and deemed too worthy by far to use. Saved for a rainy day.

Ha, the last laugh's on me, isn't it?

An inclement season has unexpectedly arrived and I have only six months to get through my stash.

So, since I'm fast approaching the finish line, I will sit awhile with these makings. These trinkets that I've saved.

I will linger and look, touch and feel. Wander about the playground of my mind. Fool around and make a mess.

I can be profligate, extravagant, and oh good goddess, even wasteful. Most of all I can, and will, play wildly.

Cataloguing can wait, but I cannot. My time has come.

The Artist Compiles Her Catalogue

What about putting pictures of my art in the catalogue that I'm assembling?

Because after the bonfire - if it comes to that - the titles of my art pieces will be meaningless. Labels of something that once was. Hell, I could even make them up. But it is the tactile two and three dimensional works themselves that are real and that photos could capture.

So images to accompany the inventory. Plus, a title and a caption that gives the technical details - materials, where, when, and perhaps why - as if any artist ever knows the reason for what they do.

Ah, there's the rub. Why did you use up your one and

only span of existence on earth applying gobs of colour to different sizes of blank canvas?

What a stupid Sisyphean way of spending your life.

What a fuck-up! What a waste!

Early on, I considered doing something else, something more worthwhile. But my imagination utterly failed me.

In reality, painting got me through just about every crisis. I truly enjoyed burning up the days in my studio; it certainly beat holding down a tedious 9-to-5 office job.

But it's all pointless, isn't it? Whether you're a doctor, lawyer or CEO, you're just putting in time. Passing your days until the end of the game.

Now then, I've selected a pristine leather-bound journal with crisp vellum pages. And I've rinsed out and filled my Montblanc pen with aqua blue ink.

I'm ready, like some hoary medieval keeper of records, to inscribe a few artworks into my *catalogue d'oeuvres*. *Le catalogue definitif.*

My, that sounds so much more cultured than inventory, doesn't it? If only the bureaucrats had a sense of *élan*.

French again. Oh well, what can I do?

Was I a closet Francophone all my life and just didn't let it out? Or maybe, I'm rehearsing for my reincarnation as a *belle artiste* or *chanteuse* crooning *"je ne regrette rien"* into the endless night.

There. I've written details on five of my works. It's taken much longer than I would have liked. Every title brought up, in an exhaustingly harrowing way, the intense feelings that I had when I created the piece.

And if that's the case with listing all of my works, I'll never get finished before my imminent deadline with the Grim Reaper. Perhaps though, like Scheherazade, I can stave off the end by adding yet one more painting to my catalogue.

If so, then surely I'm wise to procrastinate and continue my ruminations about my past art. Besides my nostalgic musings may give me some insight and a clearer perspective on what my life's journey was all about.

Already I realize that my striving days are over.

I have to complete my inventory, yet I don't feel unduly stressed about this self-directed task. Just a great exhaling. A cathartic letting go. Absolute resignation, I suppose.

If I had held that attitude early on, I would have felt a lot less *Sturm und Drang* as I went about my paltry business of making art. For in the end, does any of it matter?

Although my ultimate fate is known through the crystal ball of medical technology, my actual days left are still virgin territory. And I can live them any way I want.

I cannot change the chapters that are already written, but I can shape the ending to my life story as I wish.

In other words, I will thumb my nose at legal rules and restrictions and use up my finite time on this sacred earth to make more art.

I will seize my paint brushes, dip them once again into vivid pigments and watch them explode on the pure white surface of yet another bare canvas.

And dare I dream, too, that working on my *pièce de résistance* will hold off the death warrant just a bit?

Why not? It's the only way to go girl!

The Artist Walks to Her Studio

My goodness, I'm finding all this meandering around my memory *cache* to be awfully unsettling.

I think that it's best if I start my *pièce de résistance* right away and not dilly-dally with self-indulgent list-making.

Let me go out the door and off for a walk to my studio. The only place in the world where I can envelop myself in blissful solitude.

As I stroll to my sanctuary, I make my usual effort to empty my mind of all the routine to-dos, the dutiful whatnots that ceaselessly tie my brain in knots.

I try to be not vacantly mindless, but rather completely mindful. Aware of every little thing I see as if I'm viewing it for the first time.

Today however, I add a novel challenge - not to mull over my impending doom and not to see everything as if for the last time.

Workers were repairing the sidewalk in front of my house last week. Amazingly organized and quick at their jobs, they finished both sides of the street in just two days.

And when they poured the wet concrete, I was so tempted to sneak out and press my hand into the fast-drying mortar. To make my mark, Bansky-like.

I didn't though. I curbed my impulse, fearing their anger and not wanting to ruin their hard work.

Memory jolt: when I was a child of about eight walking with my mother to the store, I set my foot in some recently poured cement on the pavement. A worker saw what I did, yelled and swiftly smoothed it over.

Mortified as only a child could be, I cried and lied, saying I was sorry and that I had slipped.

My mother moved on and I followed. Yet every time I passed that way, and it was often as it was the only route to the grocery store, the shoemaker's and the dry goods shop, I felt ashamed of what I had done.

Though I knew that the act and the ensuing lie were only

venial sins, no amount of confessing would alleviate my embarrassment.

Now is the first time that I've related this incident. The shame of my childhood transgression is still buried deep within me.

So this morning on my way to the studio, I pay attention to the world beneath my feet. And I notice the dandelions growing out of the cracks, the poorly repaired tar patches, and the accessibility ramps at the corners where sidewalk meets street.

I carefully count my steps and then I lose track as I notice the charming way that workers have laid bricks, instead of concrete, around the base of a tree whose roots have taken over half the walkway.

I see the tiny footprints of a cat impressed in the cement on the edge of an alleyway. And I stop and smile.

Clever cat - she got to leave her mark! And lucky me, I managed to spot it and laugh at the absurdity of trying to make anything perfect - even a piece of pavement.

It struck me that the paw prints enhanced that dull patch of grey cement. It made me want to do a little dance of delight. Sheer whimsy.

What more could one ask for on a morning's walk?

Leaving our mark. Isn't that what we do when we make something?

We want to howl like Ginsberg at the uncaring cosmos and pierce the void by showing that we were here and that our being in this place matters.

But is it really necessary that we create some tangible thing - a painting, a song lyric, a piece of pottery - that may survive our demise?

Yet if not, why are we seemingly hard-wired to create?

What urge compelled our ancestors to scratch and stain their cave walls?

What drove Homer to relate the epic tales of *The Iliad* and *The Odyssey*?

Was it a collective of artists or a lonely shepherd who incised the puzzling Nazca lines into the landscape of Peru?

Those stylized spiders, monkeys, fish, llamas, lizards and human figures were etched on such a mammoth scale that it wasn't until airplanes first flew over South America in the 1920s that they were recognized.

What was that, if not leaving sacred marks on Mother Earth for the universe to see?

The tombs of Egypt, the mystery of Stonehenge, the paintings of Picasso, the sculptures of Barbara Hepworth.

My mind boggles at humankind's endless creativity. And my heart breaks when I wonder about all the marvellous creations yet to be.

Damn the finiteness of life and the profanity of death!

My life, my death!

I am not religious in the traditional sense of adhering to a specific faith, but I like to think that I am a spiritual being. I see these indications of the human spirit and feel their sacredness profoundly.

Although I do not worship these gestures made visible, I do venerate them. I stand in awe before the power of art and bow down in homage to the artists.

I do the same with nature, and not just in front of the exceptional and monumental. I also genuflect before the ordinary. I marvel at a pebble, the bark of a tree, and yes, a cat's paw prints hardened in cement.

This reminds me of an interview I gave long ago. I said something about highlighting fragments of a greater whole.

That I wanted to entice viewers to look at everyday things in a more perceptive way. I wanted people not only to see, but also to appreciate the sacred in the profane.

I thought at the time that showing different ways of seeing would help restore beauty and caring into what I then felt was a drab and indifferent world.

Pretentious art-speak drivel, I suppose. Full of youthful naivety. Still, I haven't changed much.

As I review and think about my life's work, I've become aware that my primary focus has always been to notice the magnificence in the mundane and to try to capture that essence in my mark-making.

Anyway, it takes me about half an hour to walk from my home to my studio which is located in a refurbished 19th century cotton mill in the north end of the city.

This area was crowded with hard-core industries - steel mills, food-processing companies, slaughter houses, meat-packing plants, glass manufacturers, and auto part fabricators - throughout the first half of the 20th century.

As the global economy shifted and manufacturing moved to Mexico, China and India, most of the factories closed their doors and abandoned their buildings.

During *The Decline*, a few, like the former mill that houses my workspace, were renovated and re-purposed for offices and for the so-called "creative industries."

As I climb the back stairs to my *atelier*, I note that the centre of each step is depressed, worn down by the tread of the hundreds of feet that tramped up and down that flight in the mill's heyday.

What stories that stairway could tell of workers hurrying to punch in before the buzzer signaled the start of a shift and of weary souls clumping down at day's end.

Perhaps too, of a handsome young man lingering at the bottom of the staircase while his lover changed out of her work clothes.

I can't help but inhale the vigorous spirit of the men and women who once worked in the cotton mill. The feeling of times past and hard physical labour permeate not just the stairway, but also the brick walls, radiators, tin ceilings and plank floors throughout the building.

I quicken my pace as I take the last few steps. Such is my anticipation and my eagerness to get there.

Unlocking the door and flipping on the lights, I stride into my magic circle, and smile.

I am here where I want to be - where I belong.

I take in the room as if for the first time, even though I have worked in this studio almost every day for the past twenty years. I put down my bag, take off my jacket and survey my work.

I haven't been here since I got the grim news and I realize how much I miss my sanctuary. For it is truly my refuge. No one is allowed in. Nobody comes here unless I invite them and I've asked few people throughout all the years.

My studio is my home in the full and heartfelt sense of every *cliché* that you can think of. I've relished this peaceful abode and when the end comes, I know that this is the place that I will grieve for, more than anywhere I've ever lived.

But perhaps peaceful is the wrong word. Painting is not a particularly serene activity. It's full of drama as pent-up emotions let loose on the canvas.

What happens in this room can be chaotic, and even violent when I slash and scratch and otherwise attempt to wrest art out of the raw stuff of life.

I expect that's what it means to be totally caught up in the act of creation. To be absolutely lost in the process. And to be wholly free not only to make, but also to destroy.

Except now I see none of that commotion.

A six by six foot hunk of raw material nailed to the wall sports a few vigorous strokes in electric blue. A hue so bright that it shocks me and I wonder why I chose that particular garish colour.

I eye the piece warily. It's still too early to determine what it means. Right now it suggests nothing to me although I do like the force of the strokes and the thickness of the paint, if not the pigment.

But I don't yet have any connection to it. No relationship. That needs time and I know it will come if I let it.

I turn around and catch sight of two smaller paintings on easels. I'd been looking at them for weeks, reluctant to say whether they were finished, unwilling to let them go.

Are they a pair? Are they connected? Does it matter?

From time to time, I try to fix something on one or the other - rub out, add a daub, adjust a colour - and then I sit and look again.

I spend a lot of time sitting and watching paint dry. I stick an uncompleted work up on the paint-splattered wall and then draw back to stare at it.

I don't know exactly what I'm looking for. Hours, days even, can pass as I try to figure out a work, to ask it what it needs and then to be quiet and wait for the reply.

Eventually though, I move in close, zeroing in like some bullfighter dancing his *pas de deux* with the dangerous beast.

A few moments later, my eyes still fixed on the painting, I back up and choose my weapon.

I select a tool not with any forethought, but haphazardly, picking up whatever my hand lights on - palette knife, rough brush, bunched up rag or even that rusty metal pasta scoop. Whatever gizmo the work tells me to use.

In much the same way, I pluck a colour from the array, or should I say disarray, on my work table and begin to make my mark.

Sounds easy, doesn't it?

Alas, it is never simple. Always a struggle. Sometimes I attack the work. Other times I caress it. I don't know why, I just do it.

Through it all, it's not me. It's the painting telling me what to do. The victim directing the perp.

Strange business this art-making.

I step back once more. Look, see something, and as often as not, change my marks.

Such is my practice, my slow laborious method.

Put on, take off; move back, gaze, consider; add a bit of this and a touch of that, remove a smidgen; shift my position, stare again.

This incessant, never-ending, conscious decision-making - do I do this or that, put in or take out, more or less, now or later - is absurdly draining, and yet revivifying.

And it feels like I never learn. I'm always putting too much on and then having a devil of a time scrubbing it off. Hours go by, and I accomplish so little.

Now, with merely months left to me, will my technique change? Will I finally master painting or will I die a student, forever green?

It's hard work this painting.

Yes, it takes a lot of physical energy and not just for the big muscle parrying and thrusting, daubing and smearing, shifting up and down, but also for the isometric state of being still, sometimes for an unbearably long time.

Of course, it requires a great deal of mental stamina as well to force oneself to stop even though you don't know what you are pausing for. And it's terribly difficult to control one's natural urge to move, to get up and to do something, anything instead of just sitting.

I admit that it takes all the brain power that I can muster to force myself to focus, to concentrate intensely on the work at hand and at the same time to free my monkey mind from its torrent of ceaseless nattering.

To not worry. To not obsess over all the other things that I could be doing if only I was not here, not now, not doing this stupid, useless activity.

Not wasting my life scrutinizing globs of colour on a piece of rough cloth.

Today, I question not just the works in progress in my studio, but the whole point of painting at all.

It's ridiculous, don't you think?

A complete waste of time. A frivolous indulgence that keeps me occupied and out of trouble.

But so what? And to what end?

I know there are no answers to these wretched queries for I've been in this desolate state before.

Typically I linger a while, immobilized and forlorn; then inevitably, I find my release in the painting.

No, not in discovering something enlightening in the piece, but rather in making the painting, in doing the work.

For ultimately, I am passionately committed to slathering a blank canvas or paper with colours and shapes and textures that will become I know not what. Except that it will, in due course, after lots of putting on and taking off, turn into something new.

Indeed, it will become a work that I will be pleased with,

at least for a moment.

And I will bask in that sudden flash, before I start the whole tortuous procedure again with fresh forms and colours and nothingness all stirred up in my restless head.

Yes, painting is my way. It lets me explore the uncharted territory of my mind and the ebb and flow of life with its endless swirling motion, its tensions and disturbances, and its richness, beauty, and incredible diversity. What Zorba the Greek called "the full catastrophe of life."

And I suppose that there are worse ways to fritter away your time. That is, when you have a lifetime to squander.

Enough. Now I need a break. Time-out from my demons.

I make a cup of tea. Look out the window at the barren courtyard below. Stare at the brick *façade* across the way. Eat an apple. Flip through a magazine. Eye my bookcase longingly.

After such an interlude, I usually wrench my eyes back to what I'm working on. Though not now, not with the Angel of Death stalking me.

I suddenly don't feel safe here in my sanctuary. I don't feel serene. I don't feel any joy. Instead I'm unfocused, on edge and terribly sad. So I don't put on my music and I don't start the dance of creativity.

I just sit and gaze vacantly at the big, almost blank canvas with the shocking blue strokes. I sip cold tea and stare at the two smaller pieces.

I think about how much time is left? And I wonder what to do? After a while, I notice that I'm cold and it's starting the get dark outside.

Weary with my day's work not done, I push myself up and put on my jacket to go home. Before I close the lights, I take a final look around my studio as if for the last time.

The Artist Walks to Her Studio Again

The next morning I wake to dazzling sunlight and all manner of visionary colours and weird shapes bopping in my brain. I quickly pack a lunch and head out.

I like taking different routes, exploring various streets and alleys, when going to the studio and back. I make a game of it and think yet again of drawing a map and colouring in all the blocks that I've walked.

For sure, I could have had loads of fun doing this and challenging myself to hike the whole north end. It's the kind of methodical task that I enjoy. Alas, now it's too late.

So I'll just have to add that little diversion to the heap of regrets I'm swiftly accumulating as my mind pivots back to the harsh fact of my grim diagnosis. It's one more thing on my bucket list that I won't achieve.

Actually that's a lie. I never did fancy making such a list even though their popularity swelled during *The Decline* when thousands of bucket blogs proliferated across the virtual universe.

One Hundred Experiences to Have Before You Kick the Bucket. Fifty Things to Do Before You Die. Eighty Places to Visit Before It's Over. Follow George as He Fills his Bucket. Mary Jane's Be-All, End-All List.

I always found such blogs to be essentially egotistical, glorified to-do lists. A way of pathetic one-upmanship as people competed to see who could score the most impressive or most outlandish projects, and then share them with their online friends.

No, this trivial whim of mine is hardly the type of thing that anyone would record.

Come to think of it though, I haven't seen many accounts

of major regrets online either.

But then, who knows? That virtual universe is vast and ever expanding.

Kick the bucket. Interesting term for dying, isn't it?

Sounds rather harsh and brutal though. With such finality to it. I really don't like the phrase at all.

Still, its etymology is curious. Thank you, Amazoogle!

I discovered that in the past they didn't hang criminals who stood on over-turned buckets by kicking the buckets out from under them.

Nor were suicides by hanging while standing on buckets that common in the middle ages when the expression was first noted.

One possibility for the origin of the saying had to do with the practice of laying out a corpse. A pail of holy water was placed at its feet, so visitors could sprinkle the deceased. Sometimes the dying person's legs would reflexively stretch, inadvertently knocking over the bucket.

Ha, one last kick at the can.

Seems a bit forced and rather suspect to me. Personally, I think that explanation is just another way for the Catholic Church to promote its dogma.

I prefer the secular and much more probable derivation of the idiom that has to do with animals.

One suggestion deals with the way that swine were killed in the middle ages. Pigs to be slaughtered were often hung upside down from a bar (*buchet* in French) to facilitate the blood draining from their bodies. In their death throes, the animals would always kick the *buchet*.

Makes sense and, needless to say, I quite like its French origins. Interesting how so many vestiges of Gallic words lie beneath the English language.

I also delight in the anthropomorphic notion about the goat kicking over its milking bucket and thereby spilling its life force - the vital liquid that is essential for it to sustain its offspring, the new generation.

What perversity on the part of that animal. And how well it suits our image of the churlish goat. Sort of a passive-aggressive rebellion that rather appeals to me.

Certainly, it begs the question of what gives humans the right not only to steal sustenance from other mammals, but to slaughter them, too.

Now as I walk to my studio, I dump the idea of a bucket-map completely out of my head, and smile wryly as I pass a bevy of buckets at the corner of every block.

Nicknamed the Magic Nine, these large containers store discarded waste materials mandated by *The Alchemy Law* for conversion into new forms. And even though I know that it's for the good of society, I can't help but be a little upset by the loss of the creative possibilities concealed in the detritus that they hold.

Unexpectedly, I recall *Walk Around the Block*, my first attempt at a work that mixed media together - photographs, painting, and found material - on a wooden support.

That funky assemblage linked pictures to a painted map of the street where I lived and incorporated into the work all sorts of bits and pieces. The kind of scraps now relegated to the Magic Nine.

I had shot the photographs over the course of a year as I tramped around that one block at different times of day - dawn, noon, late afternoon and dusk - and in every season.

I documented things like the view from the railroad overpass many times. Sometimes I took a particular image, such as the restaurant sign with the missing letter that read

Go-d Eats, only once.

Occasionally, when I went back to retake a photo, it had totally disappeared. Obliterated without a trace as if it had never existed.

Except I knew that it had been there. And I had proof, for I had captured its reality in a photo.

For this project, I used a Polaroid camera that produced one-of-a-kind printed pictures instantly. At the time, way before digital cameras, preview screens and Instagrams, that innovative process was truly magical.

I remember what fun I had strolling that block. I never found it tedious or uninteresting in the least as there was always something novel to photograph and to discover.

What's more, on my wanderings I had gleaned quite an array of odd fragments, some of which I positioned around the map on the finished piece.

Now that I think of it, that's possibly where my idea of colouring a map of my latest routes stems from. So perhaps I needn't regret not doing it as I've come full circle.

I have, in fact, already completed that activity in my long ago *Walk Around the Block* artwork.

And with this insight, I can now better appreciate the closing words in T. S. Eliot's *Four Quartets* poem:

"We shall not cease from exploration and the end of all our exploring will be to arrive where we started and know the place for the first time."

Feeling energized by my brisk walk and with thoughts of transformations twirling around in my head, I arrive at my destination.

I barely get my jacket off before I flip on my battered old music box and scroll to Joni Mitchell's poignant ballad, *The Circle Game*.

Soon I'm choking back tears and singing the chorus along with her. Joni reminds me that life cycles in an endless loop. We can't regain the past; we can only go on with the game.

I play the song continuously, and before too long, I find myself touching up one of my smaller canvases.

I see where I can add a bit of Payne's grey and a few dashes of yellow ochre. Then I stand back and look at the whole again. Maybe a tad of crimson and a few strokes of white. No, not good. Wipe that splotch away.

Take it slow, Lena. You have all the time you need to spend on just this one piece. You have nothing else to do, nowhere else to go. Nothing to accomplish, but to be here now, intensely alive, with this work.

After a while I make myself a coffee and eat my lunch. As I chomp on carrot sticks, my eyes return to the canvas and I immediately know what to do.

Carrot down, paint brush up, I uncap a tube of burnt sienna and move in. Another bite and forest green calls out to me. Mix in some medium and retarder and I'm off.

Before I realize it, the painting is no longer what it was. The earlier strokes are absorbed, transmuted like water to wine. I am nowhere near finished, but I have begun.

And so, I will go round and round this work in sort of a circle game for many more days. However many it takes to complete it.

I know that I'm being rather liberal with time. But when I envision that heavy black door at the end of the corridor, it is closed. Still firmly shut. I think it's locked although I do check it nightly as I struggle to sleep.

And when I see it's finally ajar, then perhaps I will begin to embrace my final transformation beyond that passageway.

For now though, I just want to hop, skip and boogie down

the corridor, flinging open all of the brightly coloured side doors that I come upon and gather up in my arms all the wondrous gifts that I find behind them.

The Artist Muses on Fate

I take a break and open *The Tibetan Book of the Dead*. No, it's not as morbid as it sounds. The book is mostly about living. Buddhists believe that contemplating one's mortality leads to an enhanced life, not just a better death.

I may have left it too late to benefit from its guidance on living; however, I sure could use some advice now about how to have a worthy ending. So I will set my brushes aside and simply read for a while.

I start by reflecting on the three certainties of the death meditation: death is inevitable, the time of our passing is unknown, and only our mental and spiritual development can help us have a good demise.

There is no possible way to escape death. I will die most likely from the cancer that I have already been diagnosed with. Although I could get killed sooner in any number of ways - in a car accident, in a plane crash or by falling down stairs, for example.

Like everyone, I've been journeying towards death since the moment I was born. For as musician Jim Morrison said, "Nobody gets out of here alive."

So it is and so it will be - the way of the world.

How long we live is uncertain. My doctor told me that I have six months based on her experience with others, yet because each person is unique, her prediction is only an estimate. An educated guess perhaps, but still not definite.

I am more optimistic. I expect at least a thousand and one

nights before I say a last *au revoir* to my studio. And there's always the possibility of a remission. In my case, it would be miraculous, but hey, miracles do occur.

Buddhists believe that when we die we leave behind our bodies, the physical manifestation that we have on earth, just like a butterfly sheds its cocoon.

So here's a big if-only that everyone should consider: if only we'd spent less mental energy fussing over our corporal being and more concentrating on our spiritual essence.

What a shameful waste of time it is, worrying about our weight and our shape. For in the end, none of that makes a difference, does it?

Confronting one's own death though is serious business. Without a doubt, it should be the most important concern anyone has in this world.

That's why, I suppose, all that Buddhist bunk matters. Still, what really counts?

For me, it's always been about making art. And that's not going to change even now. Painting enriches my psyche and feeds my soul. The only thing that does. Therefore, I will carry on and make more art.

Regrets? I have only one - my unmade works. Incubating eggs that will never hatch.

So be it. Out of my control.

For now, I will get on with the dance, blissfully painting as much as I can until I'm done. Play on *maestro*, play on....

The Artist Endures

Reading *The Tibetan Book of the Dead* focused me. And over the next days which soon turned into months, I showed up in my refuge and painted. Often in a frenzy as if time itself was running out, for it definitely was.

During that frantic period, my usual intense way of working became increasingly obsessive.

At first, I diligently set about fixing several small pieces that were lying about my studio. And in a meditative stupor, I completely lost myself in finishing them.

After that dreamy lull, my attention soon turned to the mega canvas nailed to the wall. The one whose vivid blue streaks had so startled me when I returned to my studio after my diagnosis.

I let loose on it and my howl turned into a big, boisterous, visceral shout-out for my being - being alive, being here, and being able to create.

I didn't think of this as my ultimate piece. It simply was what it was: another painting that needed resolving. And I believe that it became a damn good one because of what went into it.

All the experiments, all the mistakes, all the horrendously wrong marks. And the split second decisions, the drawn out debates. The colours that did, then didn't work, then did again. The mishmash of sand, kitty litter and ashes that I mixed into the paint, applied and then scraped off. The *mélange* of broken sea shells and sparkly metal sequins, that at various times, I both randomly strewed and meticulously positioned on the canvas.

Ugh. It sounds like I created a mess, and I expect I did - a wonderful chaotic hodgepodge of a thing that probably only its mother could love.

Nonetheless, the painting had somehow come together. And the multiple layers of hidden marks and endless rub-outs seeped into what had been electric blue, transforming it into something quite unique, and rather special.

193

I can't tell you how long I worked on, or I should say played with, this piece and it really doesn't matter.

Making it gave me so much heartfelt delight. A rich joy that was unsullied by gloomy thoughts.

Yes, the pure act of painting became my ritual salve. A holistic medicine *par excellence* that allowed me to be blissfully oblivious to my uncertain future.

And accompanying my ecstatic frolic, and surely adding enormously to my idyll, was non-stop blaring music.

For in order to create anything, especially at this time, I needed to be completely out of my mind, and music, my drug of choice, helped get me there.

Now I'll tell you something about the tunes that attended this wild spree of art-making - the melodies that I listened to as I fooled around in my studio.

I would usually begin with a good dose of Miles Davis to get myself centred. And then if I was feeling kind of blue, I would go deeper with songs from that mournful balladeer, Leonard Cohen.

Weird transition, crazy choice, makes no sense. But hey, who cares? I liked it and that's all that counts.

And truthfully, not all of Cohen's songs were downers. I think of *Dance Me to the End of Time, Boogie Street*, and yes, that great hymn, *Hallelujah*, that I played so frequently it became my earworm *du jour* more often than not.

Leonard and I go way back. I think he may have been the one constant musical love of my life, spanning my university days to my now ending days.

I was a fan before it was fashionable, way ahead of the era of poets as pop idols, long before celebrity-mania.

The first time I heard him, he was giving a reading from *Parasites of Heaven*, his early book of poems. Leonard's singing would come later. And then I would listen to him chant his songs of love and hate so repetitively that I wore out the grooves on more than one record.

Anyway, after this indulgence, I would rev myself up with honky-tonk piano music, or classic rock and roll.

I won't say that my tastes changed in these waning days of my life as I was reluctant to seek out new voices, wanting so terribly to hear my beloved favourites one more time.

Accordingly, I continued to play the music that I enjoyed the most. Because many tunes were by singers who had died young - troubled souls like Billie Holiday, Janis Joplin and Amy Winehouse - my sense of their brief lives was heightened and I found that I couldn't listen to them without also thinking of their tragic endings.

Reflecting on the self-destructive waste of those young lives made me sadder than I thought I could be. Yes, even more down-hearted than pondering my own *finale*.

Yet oddly enough, along with this feeling of melancholy came a sense of energy. I felt uplifted by their talent and thankful that they had brazened out the challenges of life long enough to accomplish what they did. And I was acutely conscious once again of the enduring power of art.

I loved those days of vigorous painting with my spirit full of an incredible freedom that I can only think came from knowing that it would end soon.

Electric Blue and the paintings that followed in a great outpouring, I titled my *Optimism of Colour* series. To create these juicy works, I used not only shocking blue, but neon pinks, brilliant reds, lime greens and mustard yellows.

Bright and breezy, in spite of what I knew about my future, these exuberant paintings shouted out my happiness at still being alive, and being able to make art. Gutsy, rash and raw, they blaze with a new-found boldness.

I will admit though that shouldas and if-onlys pursued me relentlessly all through this madcap process.

And in all honesty, from time to time, my fears and my forebodings crushed my spirit, and stopped me cold.

But this was infrequent and when it happened, I would call it a day, go for a brisk walk, and later indulge in creamy dark chocolates and fizzy *Champagne*.

Then after a good night's sleep, I would return to my sanctuary and start to play some more.

This was life, life worth living, my life now.

Going to my studio was, I confess, an escape not only from mulling over my foreshortened future, but also from gathering and reviewing my artwork.

In the evenings, after a glass or two of wine, I tried to go through my exhibition catalogues and the art that I had at home. But this mostly made me cry, and I can't say that I accomplished much.

Sometimes I would start making a list of the places where I had stashed my work, except I didn't get very far there either. I seemed to have lost the impetus to proceed with anything boring or trivial, even my *catalogue definitif*.

Summing up my life in an inventory exercise felt utterly pointless, and dreadfully final.

I just wanted to keep on painting, not look back to review and count. I didn't like to think of myself as an artist past her prime, never mind at the end of her days.

I continued to delve into *The Tibetan Book of the Dead*, both in my studio and at home. And like a good student of Buddhism, I repeatedly read the description of the death process. Rehearsing, in fact, my demise.

This meditation is supposed to make us more familiar

with, and less afraid of, dying.

And since I didn't have any other spiritual practice, this seemed as good a task to undertake (no pun intended) as any other. Only time will tell if it calms my fears.

Advanced practitioners of death simulation - whoa is that kinky! - are apparently no longer subject to uncontrolled death and rebirth like us ordinary folk.

For them, it is essential to know the eight stages of dying and the mind-body relationship behind those junctures.

As for me, I had always thought control to be a defect and while I'm fine with just waiting for the real thing as it hovers nearby - no rush, mind you - I was a tad curious about the path that lay ahead.

Although maybe I only wanted to follow the girl-scout motto: *Be Prepared.*

I found the depiction of the close signs of death such as the dissolution of the four elements - earth, water, fire, and air - fascinating in a spiritual, more than macabre, way.

And the auras surrounding the phases of mind when dying - progressing from white to red to black to clear - appealed to my visual sensibilities, and inspired me.

So while musing on my upcoming rendezvous with the Great Leveller, I worked for many weeks on a vast canvas nailed to my studio wall.

When I finally completed it, I found that I had created a painting that embodied in colour and form the eight stages, the last breath, and the release of the body in death.

I don't know if *Release* communicates any of that sweet mystery to anyone else, or if it's just my secret vision. Still, seeing it hanging on the wall next to my bed before I go to sleep each night moves me greatly.

Much more than that horrid little prayer that I was taught

as a child to say at bedtime: "Now I lay me down to sleep, I pray the Lord my soul to keep, but if I die before I wake, I pray the Lord my soul to take."

That invocation was certainly guaranteed to give one a lifetime of fear-induced insomnia, I'll say!

Is *Release* my *pièce de résistance*? Who knows?

It's not my last though, for I had no sooner finished it than I created another large work that I find awesome.

Life After Death is abstract too, but I see in it a massive outline of a structure or a mammal perhaps.

A sea-monster or a whale covered with rusty undersea forms - barnacles, lichen and coral - that live and flourish on decomposing matter.

And now, after adding these two pieces to my catalogue, I tack up yet another canvas, face the wall, and begin again.

About the Author

Linda Joyce Ott is a writer and artist. *The Naked Law* is her first novel. Her collection of short stories, *Open Wounds, Secret Obsessions,* was published in 2013.

Linda lives in Hamilton, Ontario, Canada with her husband Günter, and two cats, Scampi and Squeak.

To see her art and photography, visit her website or blog www.lindajoyceott.com   www.optimismofcolor.com

Made in the USA
Charleston, SC
11 July 2015